RETURN TO SENDER

INVITATION TO EDEN SERIES
BOOK 1 IN *SUMMER IN LOVE* SERIES

STEENA HOLMES

DEDICATION

This story is for all you chocolate lovers out there who understand the pain of losing your soul mate. May you find happiness, may your soul be blessed and may you never stop searching…

CHAPTER ONE

A delicious box of handmade chocolates from one of the best chocolatiers in the world sat on her desk. They were his latest creation and he wanted her to taste test them for him. Damn that man. Paul Ormand, her friend from her college days and now a world—renowned chocolatier, knew she was trying to lose weight. She could have sworn he did this on purpose.

"A sweet thank-you for all you do, my foot," she muttered to herself. He'd called in a favor a few months ago and she'd been able to help him. When he'd asked what he could do to repay the favor, she'd jokingly suggested chocolate but then told him she was still on her diet and if he sent any she'd make him pay.

She should have known better.

The tantalizing aroma from the opened box tempted her and it was all she could do not to try one. The smart thing would be to close the box, put it away in a drawer and attempt to forget about them.

"Oh, what do you have there?" Melanie, her sister, peered over her shoulder and went to reach for one of the decadent pieces of heaven.

"Hands off." She slapped the offending hand away and glared up at her sister, who smirked and stuck her tongue out at her.

"I do just as much for the man and he doesn't send me chocolates." Melanie pulled a chair up to Lauren's desk.

"He loves me more," Lauren teased.

"That's only because he met you first."

"Or maybe he still remembers you trying to fool him into thinking you were me?"

Lauren was the oldest of triplets and despite having the same facial features of both her sisters, Melanie was the only one who had the same body type, or close to it. Jessica, the youngest of the three, could pass for a model.

Melanie shrugged before she reached over and snagged a chocolate despite Lauren's glare.

"Are you or are you not a diet?"

"I am," Lauren grumbled.

"Well then," she popped the chocolate into her mouth, "conshider jist my way of helfing," Melanie said with a full mouth.

Lauren shook her head before she inhaled the decadent smell that came from the box. Somehow she managed to replace the lid and move the box out of reach...but it was difficult. One chocolate normally wouldn't hurt, but she'd been so good lately and was down twelve pounds. Just another twenty or so to go and she'd maybe go swimsuit shopping. Maybe.

"Have you heard from Jess today?" Melanie licked the chocolate off her fingers before she leaned back in her chair and crossed her legs.

"Not yet." Lauren checked the time. "She said she'll call when she gets to her room tonight."

"What venue was she checking out today?"

Lauren grabbed a notebook from the side of her desk and thumbed through the pages until she found the itinerary she'd written out.

"Today was that surprise day Lexi and Paul asked to have free." She had some ideas where they were headed, hints Paul had given her on the phone.

"And she comes home when, again?" Melanie pulled out her phone.

"Two more days. Haven't you booked her return flight yet?"

Melanie's lips pursed. "No and I'm starting to get a little worried. Not only is the flight more expensive now but she hasn't responded to any of my emails or texts in the past few days."

Lauren's chest tightened for a brief moment until she remembered something. "She's using a credit, right? She'll probably just book the return flight at the airport. You got that email when I gave her the return options, right?" When Melanie nodded, Lauren smiled. "Nothing to worry about then."

"We're talking about Jess, right? Our baby sister who tends to leave things to the last minute? The one who misses flights all the time? Who only thinks of herself at the best of times?"

"The same one who is the most adventurous, who can sweet-talk her way out of any situation and always finds the most amazing deals for us. Yes, that one." Lauren preferred to give Jess the benefit of the doubt. It was easier on her nerves.

Melanie leaned forward. "Do you know for sure she's with Lexi and Paul? For sure sure? Remember that time she ditched the tour guide, paid him to lie to us and took off for a week, suntanning on some beach?"

Lauren winced. "Yeah, but the Jennings loved that trip afterwards, didn't they? If it hadn't been for her doing that, we never would have found that secluded beach."

Melanie shook her head in disgust but Lauren attempted to ignore it.

"At least this chocolate tour will be what our happy bride is looking for." Melanie reached for a stack of mail Lauren had dropped into a basket and flipped through it.

Lauren almost groaned. In the five years of operating Bella Dia as an exclusive travel concierge, they'd seen a lot. Their clientele were the elite, the rich, and extremely privileged for the most part. Lauren and her sisters were known for performing miracles for those with high demands.

They currently worked with a bride and her soon-to-be husband: a wedding in Banff, Canada, nestled among the mountains, and then a honeymoon in Europe, where they wanted to take an exclusive and private chocolate tour. But not just any tour, one that was tailored exclusively to them.

That's where Paul and Lexi came in. Paul and Lexi had connections to the best chocolatiers and pastry chefs in Europe and despite Lexi leaving Paris due to a broken heart, Lauren had worked her magic to bring the two lovers back together.

Lexi was one of her best friends and she would move heaven and earth to see her back together with Paul, another good friend of hers.

It was a win-win situation. The two were back together and Lauren had a tour guide for her bride. Now, if she could only ensure the wedding went off without a hitch.

That's where Melanie and Tessa came in.

"Have you heard back from Tessa regarding the

guest list issues?"

Melanie tossed some fliers into the garbage. "I have a call scheduled in an hour."

"How many guests are we over?"

"We managed to get Ellen to narrow down her guest list by five. We're still ten over our limit and the hotel isn't budging."

"So we go to Plan B?" Ellen, the bride, wasn't too accommodating when it came to paring down her guest list. Everyone was crucial to her happiness, it seemed. Which meant if they couldn't get the hotel to overlook the five guests who may not arrive despite being invited, they had to either find a different venue or plan an outdoor wedding on the grounds of the Banff Springs Hotel.

"Plan B it is. You know, when I finally get married, I want a very quiet wedding in Mom and Dad's backyard. No fuss. No drama." Melanie leaned forward and Lauren noticed an envelope she held in her hands.

"You say that now, but when your big day comes, you can't tell me you won't want to say your vows on the beach of your favorite resort?" She glanced over at Melanie's office, where she had a wall plastered with all the locations they used for their company that she was determined to vacation at. The ones she'd visited all had postcards attached to them.

"For the honeymoon, sure. I know Jess would

rather elope but you want the intimate wedding too, right?"

Lauren shrugged. She'd never really thought much about her own wedding. Six years ago, she'd met her soul mate while on a life-changing trip to Europe, only to come home brokenhearted. If there was one thing Lauren believed in with her whole heart, it was soul mates. Her parents were the perfect examples of this to her, and she wasn't willing to settle for anything less. Even if it meant she remained single for the rest of her long and lonely life.

"In Mom and Dad's backyard and have to compete with you? Not on your life," Lauren teased. "We had another inquiry today, did you see it?" Lauren tried to get Melanie off the topic of their own weddings. The anniversary of when she first met Marc was coming up in a few days and like every other year, she was feeling a tad bit emotional. Normally she went away for a few days around this time, to reflect, to remember but this year with Jess gone, she didn't want to leave Melanie all alone to deal with Ellen.

The thought of Marc and when she'd first met him hit her hard and she bent down in a pretence to pick up her purse but in reality blinked her eyes to stop the tears from being noticeable. She hated how much it hit her, still, after all this time. The ache in her heart, the memory of his smile and the way she felt when she'd been in his arms...she only allowed herself to dwell on the memories of that intense love once a year.

"A new one? Can we handle it? I thought we'd discussed taking a month off after Ellen's wedding?" Melanie toyed with the envelope in her hand before she handed it to Lauren.

"If I was to tell you it was one of the biggest stars in Hollywood, would you say no?"

With the envelope in her hands, she fingered the linen paper and knew it was of high quality. There was no return information, just *LS* embossed in gold lettering. She turned it over in her hands and looked at Melanie.

"Who is this from?"

Melanie shrugged. "You got me. It's your initials though, I think. That L could be a J too...open it up and check."

Lauren set the envelope back down. If it was for Jess, she didn't want to intrude. But there was something familiar about the envelope, something she'd seen somewhere. She filtered through the various magazines she'd read, online sites she visited on a regular basis and that's when it hit her.

On one site's private email group she was in, a travel agent had mentioned a client receiving an envelope similar to what she held in her hand.

"Oh sweet..." She reached for Melanie's hand and held tight. "This is an invite to Eden," she said.

Melanie sat up straight. Eden was a destination

they'd talked about in the quiet morning hours as the place they would go to if they could, as the one location they wouldn't ever share with their clients...it was their nirvana, their heaven...their genie in a bottle. Invitations to the island were rarely issued, so the fact Lauren held one in her hands was a miracle in itself.

"What did Jess do to get this?" Lauren mumbled. Part of her was amazed that her sister would get the hallowed invite but then there was another part of her that was jealous...when would it be her turn? While her sisters traveled the world and fell in and out of love, Lauren was here, in this office, behind this desk, and worked to ensure everyone else's dreams came true but her own.

She reached for the box of chocolates she'd resisted earlier.

Life sucked sometimes.

CHAPTER TWO

Marc paced the room, from one end to the other. Nervous energy coursed through his body.

"If you don't sit down, we're going to leave."

Marc glared at Paul, who sat off in the corner with Lexi. They snuggled together on a large love seat, totally immersed in themselves while he sweated buckets as he waited, no, needed confirmation that everything was in place.

"Why haven't we heard yet? Are you sure it's all going to work out? Why hasn't he—" Marc was in a panic but stopped what he was about to say when he caught the glare coming from Paul.

"It's all taken care of. You need to relax."

Marc sat down on a chair and leaned forward. His elbows rested on knees that bounced.

"You asked, I delivered. My...friend...assured me the invitation would be delivered, today."

Lexi sighed. "And when he says delivered, he means we've already gotten the text that it arrived and Lauren has it. You just need to get ready for your flight and stop worrying."

Marc ran his hands through his already messy hair. His teeth ground as he swallowed back his frustration. Stop worrying? Right. Six years ago, he'd made the biggest mistake of his life and had spent years trying to mask that pain by playing a role of being a playboy—a role he played quite well, if he were honest. He'd almost forgotten about her, forgotten why that hole in his heart remained, until Lexi showed him that photo. That's when he knew...fate had given him a second chance at love and it was out of his hands.

And he was to stop worrying?

"What if she doesn't read the invitation in time? What if she doesn't get on the plane? What if all of this has been for nothing?" He jumped to his feet and paced in a circle, the worry too much for him to handle.

"It's all taken care of," Paul said.

Marc turned. "But how? How have you taken care of it? I need to know. Who is this friend of yours with such pull? How does he even have an island I've never heard about till recently and we've never been?"

Paul shrugged. "The guy has a lot of money and asked me to keep quiet. And we've haven't been because we don't need to. When and if we do, we will." When he turned his attention away from Marc to Lexi and stared into her eyes, Marc almost wanted to gag.

He was happy the two lovebirds were back together. It made his life so much easier. It had been hell to have his two best friends so at odds. Things weren't perfect yet—Lexi refused to move back to Paris—but he knew Paul would wear her down. That or he'd move to Banff, some godforsaken beautiful backwoods town just to make her happy. Marc was okay with it, except, Banff was cold and he didn't do cold.

"But what's his name? I'd rather not be made to look the fool when I arrive and don't even recognize him." Marc glanced at his watch. He had an hour before he needed to leave for his transatlantic flight.

"Oh, you won't meet him." Paul stood from the couch. "He's an old friend from school and I haven't even seen him in...way too many years. We talk via email or text only. And if anything, you'll hear people refer to the *Master*, instead of his real name. He's, well, he's a bit eccentric."

Marc slapped his forehead. "He's the dude you've been sending boxes of chocolates to every month? The one in our system labelled Eden Master? I thought that was for accounting, but it's just his name."

Paul smiled. "He loves the chocolate and places it in some of the guests' bedrooms when they first arrive."

"He must love them. It's not every day you grant exclusivity to one of your best-selling products." Marc glanced at his watch again.

"Come on." Paul must have noticed. "Let's get you to the airport."

"Just think, Marc. In a few short hours, you'll see Lauren again." Lexi stepped to his side and reached for his hands. "I just wish I had put two and two together earlier. Imagine, my best friend in the States and my best friend in Paris...I'm so happy for you guys!"

"Don't pop the bubbly, just yet," Marc grumbled. "If she doesn't get on that plane and come to the island, I'm not sure what I'll do."

"Of course you do. You'll go to the States and show up at her office. I'll even take you there myself." Lexi grabbed him in a hug. "Now, stop worrying, you big lug, and grab your luggage."

Marc already had his bag by the front door, so he waited for Lexi to grab her purse. Paul held the door open and sneaked in a kiss as Lexi passed by him.

"So, the Master, huh?" Seemed like an odd name to be called. "Master of what?"

"Just go with it. It started out as a nickname between him and his pilot and then it just caught on."

"So he's not into any of that kinky sex stuff, right?"

The look on Paul's face said it all.

"Seriously, dude?"

Paul pushed him out the door. "Are you going there to reconnect with Lauren or are you wanting to be introduced to the man in charge? You can't have both."

Marc didn't bother to reply. They both knew the answer to that.

He still couldn't believe it had taken him this long to put two and two together. Paul had mentioned Lauren numerous times to him in their meetings regarding events that were coming up. At the time, all Marc had known was that Lauren was an old friend and she tended to call in favors here and there for her company. She would always call Paul directly if she had clients coming to Paris, and Marc never thought to ask for more in-depth information about the woman.

Until Paul came home with Lexi in tow and they showed him pictures. Before coming back to Paris, they'd flown to the States to meet with Lauren personally to discuss this new venture for Lexi. Apparently, Lauren and Lexi were best friends, which boggled his mind. Paul and Lexi were his best friends,

Lauren his soul mate and yet they'd never crossed paths in the past six years.

The moment he'd seen the image of Lexi and Lauren together on a beach, it was as if he'd been punched in the gut.

Lauren, *his* Lauren, stole his breath away in that image. She'd been beautiful six years ago when they were just kids, but now, she was breathtaking. And the moment he'd seen her, all those emotions he'd bottled away came back with a force that left him reeling.

He'd convinced himself she was married with a family, that she was happy and satisfied, that she'd moved on from him...but she hadn't. And it was that knowledge—she hadn't forgotten him—that forced him to move.

It was Paul's idea to surprise her with a trip to Eden after Lexi confirmed Lauren was a workaholic who never left the office. He couldn't believe that. When they'd been together, she had a passion for traveling; it was the main reason she'd left him behind—to do what he couldn't. Back then, he'd had to stay close to home, close to his ill parents. They'd made a pact to reunite, to meet up and not let what was happening between them fizzle, but that's exactly what they'd done.

Well, to be fair, that's what he'd done.

The fact they lost touch was all his fault. He'd been the one to get scared. He just hoped he could make it up to her.

Six years wasn't a long time, really. But, back then he'd only been a kid. A stupid one who thought his life was about to end after meeting his soul mate. He'd been too young to fall in love. Or so he'd thought.

He'd made the wrong choice back then, but now he had the opportunity to correct it. And she would forgive him; she had to. At least, he hoped she would. But, there was one thing he'd learned about Lauren: expect the unexpected.

CHAPTER THREE

Eden. That hallowed island all covet to visit. And her sister was the one who ended up invited. Her sister. The one who does the most traveling. Lauren picked up another piece of chocolate and popped it in her mouth. The one who gets to experience the lifestyle their clients both crave and demand. Her sister who...probably deserved it. How could she be upset or jealous about that?

When they started Bella Dia, they'd all agreed upon their own roles. Lauren was the one with the best organizational skills, so it only made sense she stayed in the office and ran the day-to-day schedule. Melanie was the creative and most business-oriented one, so she handled the contracts, the payments, and other stuff that crept up. And Jessica, baby Jessica, was the bubbly one with a thirst for adventure that outdrove Lauren's own passion. Jess hated being in the office: she was happier to travel, visit the sites, and create relationships with the owners, the clients, and everyone else who ended up loving her and signing with them.

Their team dynamic made sense, even if Lauren grumbled about it. She'd made the decision to squash that travel bug. She'd had to and her sacrifices had more than made it worth it. Look where their company was now? They regularly ran a profit in the millions, had the cream of the crop when it came to clients and were known as *the* travel concierge. Exactly what they'd set out to accomplish.

Lauren stood, invite in hand, and went to place it in Jessica's inbox on her desk when Melanie stopped her.

"What are you doing?"

"Leaving it for Jess. Why?"

Melanie stood. "You have to open it."

"No I don't."

"Yes, yes you do." Melanie came over and grabbed the invite out of her hands. Lauren snatched it back. They played a game of tug-of-war with the invitation until Lauren gave up.

"You have to open it, Lauren," Melanie insisted. She shoved the invite into Lauren's face.

"I'm not opening Jess's invite." She took the paper

and set it down in her box and walked away.

"What if it's time-sensitive? We've both heard the rumors."

Lauren stopped and slowly turned. A sick twist in her stomach forced her to head back to Jess's desk. Rumors were that the invites were for a specific time and date and that was it. No second chances and no re-invites.

She'd really hate for Jess to miss this chance all because they never opened the invite.

"Okay, we'll open it and then send her a text to let her know when she has to be home by, deal?"

Melanie shrugged. "If she'll even check her messages, but sure."

Lauren reached for her letter opener and carefully slid it along the edge. She didn't want to destroy the envelope. This was something they'd keep, maybe mount on their wall as proof that not only did Eden exist but that Bella Dia was invited.

Melanie leaned over her as she slowly slid out the parchment paper inside and read the words imprinted on the page. She had to read them a few more times before she handed it over to Melanie.

"That says today, right?" She had to have read it wrong. She must have read it wrong. There was no way the elegant and flowy script on that paper said to meet the pilot at their small coastal airport within the hour.

"Lauren, the plane is leaving in forty-five minutes." There was a weird look in Melanie's gaze and Lauren didn't like it. She'd seen that look far too many times.

"No. No. You are not going to pretend you're Jess and go in her place. You can't." Lauren snatched the invite out of Melanie's fingers.

"They're never going to know," Melanie hedged. A sly smile crept along her face and she took a step towards Lauren, who promptly took a step backwards.

"I'll know. You'll know. Jess will know when she gets back. You can't do it. You just can't." She shook her head and clutched the invite tight to her chest.

Every time one of them attempted to swap places with another, it always ended up in ruins. Always. Although their facial features were similar, their body figures were not. And even though the pilot wouldn't know who was who—Lauren would know.

"Well, of course I can't. I'm too busy here in the office. But you could."

Everything in Lauren screeched to a halt at her sister's words. *She could?* Of course she couldn't. She didn't do that. She never did that. The last time she'd pretended to be Melanie, she'd got caught red-handed by Melanie's date and felt like a fool. Of course she wouldn't do it.

"I'm too busy as well." Her chin lifted as if to emphasise her words.

Melanie only laughed at her.

"Chicken."

Lauren's eyes widened. "Am not."

"Are too. You hide behind your desk day in, day out, year after year and barely live your life the way you used to." Melanie took another step. "You deserve some time away. Relax and enjoy yourself for once. It's Eden. The one place we've always wanted to go...no one will even know you."

Lauren shook her head. "I do too live my life," she protested. She did. She ran a successful company with her sisters and she went for long walks along the beach at night. Okay, so maybe she walked that shoreline alone but still—at least she went. And she volunteered on the weekends when they didn't have any client emergencies at the local retirement home. She had a life. And was quite happy with it.

"Neither one of us is going." Lauren put her foot down.

"What about the pilot?" Melanie asked.

"What about him?"

Melanie reread the invitation. "Says here the pilot will be waiting."

"So?"

"So, we can't just let them sit there, wondering if Jess will ever show up or not."

"Why not?" That's exactly what Lauren had planned to do. The airport was on the other side of

21

town and she had emails to respond to.

"Seriously, Lauren? What does that say about Bella Dia? At least go out to the airport and explain the situation. Maybe Jess will get re-invited." Melanie leaned against Lauren's desk, folded her arms and stared at her.

Melanie really expected her to go and do this? Why?

"I'm a little busy today. Why don't you go?"

Melanie grinned. "Sure. I can do that. No promises I'll come straight back, though. A weekend away on an exotic island sounds like—"

"Fine," Lauren interrupted her. "I'll go." She caught the satisfied gleam in her sister's eye. "On second thought, we'll both go." For some reason, she didn't trust Melanie and would rather have her by her side than left alone to her own devices. Who knows what she'd do while Lauren was out of the office.

"Fine by me." Melanie pulled her car keys out of her pocket, looped them around her finger and headed towards the main door. "If we leave now, we'll have time to stop for a coffee. The least we can do is buy one for the pilot for his return flight home."

Lauren grabbed her purse, turned off her monitor and followed after Melanie. At the door, she stopped and checked to make sure she had the invitation with her before she locked the doors behind them. She had a feeling they wouldn't be coming back anytime soon.

A single charter plane sat on the tarmac with its side door open.

As they drove closer, someone jumped out of the plane and stood there.

"See, I told you they would be waiting." Melanie smiled in satisfaction as they pulled up to a stop. Lauren just rolled her eyes. The whole ride out here, Melanie went on and on about how she couldn't believe someone from Bella Dia actually received an invite and how they shouldn't pass up the opportunity and Lauren continued to remind her that what she suggested would not happen.

Would not. End of story.

"Why don't you wait here and I'll take the coffee over and explain everything." Melanie winked at her from the driver's seat.

"Are you kidding me?"

"What?"

Lauren shook her head, knowing full well Melanie knew exactly what she meant. Her sister would do it. She'd get in that plane and go to the island without any qualms.

"I'll go." She reached for the coffee and pushed open her door.

"Make sure to take your purse." Melanie leaned

over and grabbed the handle to her bag and held it up. Lauren snatched it, flung it over her shoulder and closed the door. She started across the pavement when Melanie called out to her to come back.

She lifted her gaze to the sky. Lauren pivoted in her heels and marched back to the car, all as she muttered foul words beneath her breath.

"What?"

"You forgot your coffee." Melanie smiled up at her sweetly.

Lauren didn't say a word as her coffee was shoved into her hands. She just turned and walked away, but not before she looked over her shoulder and childishly stuck her tongue out at Melanie.

She caught the grin and fought to not smile back. As much as her sister annoyed her, she loved her and knew they'd laugh about all this on the way back to the office later.

Maybe she'd prove her sister wrong about not living her life and suggest they drive into the city for a girl's night out? Rent a hotel room at the small boutique they both loved, go to dinner at the new French restaurant that recently opened and watch the new sci-fi movie that came out.

"You must be Ms. Summers." The pilot walked towards her, a smile on her face, and held out her hand to shake.

Lauren handed her the coffee instead.

"I'm one of them, but not the one you're here for."

"Is that right?" The female pilot looked her up and down and then pulled out a photo from her breast pocket and examined it. "I'm pretty sure this is you." She turned the photo around and Lauren stared back at herself.

That didn't make sense. The invitation was for Jessica. Not her.

"You're here for Jessica, my younger sister. There's been a mix-up. We're—"

"Triplets. Yep, I know. I'm Joely, your pilot, and we're on a bit of a schedule, so if you wouldn't mind hopping on board, we can get going." Joely turned and held the door to the plane open for her.

"But I...no, there's been a mistake."

"No, ma'am. The Master doesn't make mistakes." Joely took a sip of her coffee. "Now this is good. Thank you for bringing me one. The owner inside," she pointed to the small office far off in the field, "offered me a cup of what they had, but I swear it was sludge." She wrinkled her nose in disgust. "There's nothing worse than bad coffee."

Lauren took a sip of her own and had to agree. When Jess was in the office, she wasn't allowed near the coffee machine.

Wait. "The Master?" Was that rumor true as well? Apparently there was this man no one ever saw who ran Eden.

"The one and only. If you've got an issue, he's the one to talk with. Come on, I've got some frozen items in the coolers in the back that will melt if we don't get up in the air." Joely held her hand out to help Lauren up into the plane, and without protesting, Lauren got in. It wasn't until she was inside that she realized what she'd done.

"Wait, I can't go. Can't you just tell him yourself?" She waited until Joely was in the cockpit.

"Nope. No can do. Don't worry. I have a trip back to the mainland in a few days, so I can bring you back home."

A few days?

"I can't wait a few days." She glanced out the window to Melanie and waved for help. Melanie only waved back and then Lauren watched in horror as her sister turned the car around and drove away.

"Wait," she called out. She could hardly hear over the roar of the engines and had to cover her ears to block out the noise. "This can't be happening," she yelled.

Headphones were shoved at her and Joely indicated she was to wear them. Lauren put them on and breathed a sigh of relief when the loudness of the plane dimmed.

"Can you hear me okay?" Joely's voice came through the speakers.

Lauren nodded.

"You have the wrong sister." Lauren attempted to make Joely understand but the woman shook her head.

"Lauren Summer?"

Lauren nodded.

"Then I have the right one."

"But how..." Lauren tried to process this all the while she watched her sister's car fade into the distance. How could this be happening to her? It was all a mistake.

She should have just stuck a *return to sender* sticker on the invitation and placed it back in the mail. This was ridiculous. She didn't even have a change of clothing with her.

"If you're worried about your clothing, don't be. Your sister packed a bag for you and it's in the back." Joely smiled at her before she taxied down the runway.

In the back? Her sister? A bag? What? Lauren rubbed her face as she tried to assimilate all of this and then pulled out her phone.

There was a text from Melanie.

Relax. I've got you covered. Go and enjoy some time away. You deserve it. And yes, this trip is meant for you.

Lauren's body shook as the realization of what her sister's words meant.

This had been planned. She was going to the island. To Eden. To the paradise she'd always dreamed of. Alone.

Her heart sped up until it hurt to breathe and she knew she was in the midst of a panic attack. She clutched at the armrests until her fingers turned white.

"Close your eyes and count to one hundred." Joely's soothing voice calmed her and she did as was suggested.

One. Two. Three areyoufreakingkiddingme. Four. Five. Six ohmygodImgoingtodie. Seven. Eight. Nine. Ten. Twenty thisisnotworkingandImgoingtokillMelanie...

"Look, we're up in the air now. Take a deep breath. Your sister didn't tell me you hated flying."

"I don't."

Joely's laughter was soft. "Could have fooled me."

Lauren listened to the woman talk as she told Lauren what to expect on their two-hour flight, how she normally flew from Miami to the island but since they were only a bit north of Miami, this worked just as well. As Joely talked, Lauren calmed until she could stare out the window into the crystal-blue waters below and not freak out.

She was going to Eden. To the island. Her. Not Jessica. A tiny bubble of excitement welled up inside at the idea. The last time she'd actually gone away for a vacation was...well...six years ago when she toured Europe. She'd kind of lost her passion after getting her heart broken. For her, in her head and heart, Europe contained the memories of Marc and a love so pure she knew there would never be another. But not only that, it carried the weight of a heart decimated by that love and she'd yet to heal.

Thankfully, Eden wasn't Europe.

Maybe this year she'd be able to put her memories to rest, say goodbye to the past and move forward. Maybe this year she wouldn't mourn a love lost but celebrate something new.

Maybe this year would be the start of an annual vacation where she celebrated a lighter heart full of life and happiness.

Maybe. She just needed to get past this year's anniversary first. The weight of that thought hurt and a tear trickled down her cheek before she could wipe it away. She rested her head back against the seat and closed her eyes. She didn't want to do this, not here. She was on her first trip in what seemed like forever, and if Eden was everything she anticipated it to be...she wasn't going to ruin this experience on the memories of a broken heart.

Who knows, maybe this trip was the start to healing her heart. Maybe it was time.

CHAPTER FOUR

"Wake up, sleepyhead," Joely said.

Lauren rolled her neck, slowly, to get the kink out from sleeping on an angle. When she opened her eyes, she gasped, amazed at the view out the window.

"Pretty awesome, right? It never gets old, trust me." Joely chuckled while Lauren leaned forward to get a better view.

Crystal-clear blue waters lapped against the beach shoreline of Eden, the white-capped waves mesmerizing until Lauren's gaze moved from the exotic beach to the castle more inland.

"Oh my..."

"Yep."

"Is that...that's not—" Lauren wished for a pair of binoculars for a better look.

"A castle? Yep." Joely's voice was full with laughter. "In the flesh, so to speak. Beautiful, isn't it? But that's not where you'll be staying."

Disappointment clouded Lauren's gaze for a brief moment until she saw the water bungalows like in the Maldives she routinely booked for clients.

"I can handle those." She pointed to the white roofs and smiled.

Joely shook her head. "Sorry, you won't be staying there either."

Lauren kept her gaze fixated on the island. If she wasn't staying in that amazing castle, or in those luxurious water bungalows, where was she staying? *Please don't say a tent in the jungle located in the middle of the island. Anything but that.* Just the idea of all the bugs set her skin crawling.

The plane angled to the left as they circled around and lowered until they were low enough to the water that Lauren could have jumped out if she'd wanted.

"There." Joely pointed ahead.

If the castle and the bungalows had made her gasp for air, where she would be staying took it away. She couldn't believe what she was looking at. White cottages led from out over the water, trailed down the sparking white beach and then inwards. One cottage stood out from the rest, however. It sat out in the middle of the ocean, on its own little island, and as they neared it, she could see that there was in fact two cottages on the tiny island with a shared pool between them. A wood deck connected the cottages to the mainland but Lauren could only imagine the peaceful retreat it must portray.

What she wouldn't give to stay in one of those cottages away from the others. It looked like pure heaven.

She must have sighed loud enough for Joely to hear because the woman chuckled before manoeuvring the plane to land in the water and then taxi up to the dock.

Lauren grabbed her bag and jumped out as soon as her door was open. She wobbled a bit on the wooden dock as it swayed beneath her and smiled in thanks as the pilot reached out to steady her.

"So now what?" Lauren looked around her and took it all in: the way the wind played with her hair, the sound of the water as it slapped against the wooden dock beside her yet caressed the sand ahead of her, the chirping of the birds off in the distant trees. But most importantly, she breathed in the air and let it cleanse her lungs.

She was here. Really here. In Eden. And it was nothing like she'd ever imagined it would be. She pinched the inside of her wrist to make sure she wasn't dreaming.

"Now, you wait for those Greek gods to come out and escort you to your home away from home. Now, you learn to relax and just soak up Eden. Let it heal you."

Those words, *let it heal you*, rang in Lauren's ears as Joely jumped back in the plane and taxied it away from the dock.

"Where are you going?" Lauren called out.

"Gotta drop the supplies off. The Master gets a bit cranky without his trail-mix." Joely winked and waved goodbye.

Lauren turned and noticed the men Joely had called Greek gods and had to admit, the girl was right. Even from a distance, the way the men moved...she enjoyed the view. The closer they came, the better it was.

"Ms. Summers, we're glad you were able to make it. I'm Trevor and this is Tyler." Trevor, the more muscular of the two, which really didn't say much as they both had arms the size of tree trunks and their pectoral muscles were clearly defined even through their shirts, pointed to Tyler.

Lauren smiled. They were identical twins. Closely cropped dark hair, sea green eyes and a smile to melt a heart, the only difference she could see between the two were their tattoos that covered their arms.

Tyler held out his arm and waited for Lauren to attempt to wrap her arm around it. She failed miserably.

"If you're ready, we'll escort you to your cabin. Our brother, Sean, is there making sure everything is ready."

"Sean?" Lauren laughed. "Let me guess, younger or older?"

"Middle," both men said at the same time.

"Triplets?"

They nodded. "Dad couldn't think of a name starting in U, so he went with T again," Trevor explained.

"I'm a triplet as well, the oldest. But my parents picked our names out of a hat." Her dad used to tell the story every year at their birthday, how they couldn't agree on names and so Mom wrote a bunch out that they'd written down and tossed them all in her dad's baseball hat and made their doctor pick out the names.

"Out of a hat, huh? That's got to be the best name story I've heard this week," Tyler said.

"This week?"

They walked down the pier; the guys' flip-flops smacked against the boards while she wore heels that clicked.

"There's a triplet gathering happening up in the main castle. You'll have to check it out if you have time," Tyler explained.

Lauren could only see the tall piers of the castle in the distance.

"Don't worry, one of us will escort you. It's a small island, but it's easy to get lost. One of us will always be close by to make sure everything runs smoothly for you."

Lauren liked the sound of that.

"So, in other words, I can leave everything in your capable hands?" Meaning, for once, she didn't have to plan anything out, prepare anything for anybody or...

"You leave everything up to us. And the Master, of course. This is your time to relax and enjoy. There's healing here and," Trevor leaned down close to her ear, "your heart needs it."

She glanced up at him, wondering how he knew. Just like Joely. How had she'd known?

"Is that why I'm here?" She knew people were only invited to Eden for a reason, or at least, it's what she'd heard. Was she here to heal her broken heart?

She couldn't think of a better way to do that. Not with the Greek gods by her side.

She couldn't stop smiling as they turned the corner and headed towards the large cottage off in the water. She hadn't wanted to hope, but this was the only path out there.

"Is that where I'm staying?" She breathed in deep and held her breath.

"Only the best. Those were our orders."

The best? Only the best? The exact phrase she used with her clients. Only the best from Bella Dia. Except, for once, instead of ensuring her clients were treated in this fashion, it was her.

She could get used to this.

As she walked between her two Greek gods—and she loved how she thought of them as *hers*—she wished her sisters were here with her to experience this. They worked just as hard as she did and she felt a little bit guilty for not being able to share it with them.

But when she saw Sean step out of the door to her cottage, that guilt flew away.

Every once in a while a girl deserved to be pampered and now it was her turn. Thank the good Lord above.

Marc waited on the tarmac for what he assumed was his charter plane to taxi down the runway.

There'd been a text on his phone to let him know his pilot would be late, which was a good thing since his own flight had been behind schedule.

The air sweltered around him and he tugged at his t-shirt, which was already plastered to his chest.

He'd take a Parisian summer over this Miami heat any day.

When the plane stopped, he reached for his bag and jogged the remaining distance between him and the pilot, who'd just stepped down.

He almost did a double take. This small thing was his pilot? Could she even see over the dashboard?

"Dude, if you give me that look one more time, you're not getting in. Got it?" The sprout had her arms crossed over her chest and frowned up at him. He would have smiled, but for some reason, he had a nagging suspicion she was serious.

"Sorry." If he said anything else, it would be too incriminating.

"Hope you weren't waiting too long." She grabbed his bag and hoisted it up into the back of the plane.

"My flight was delayed, so only a few minutes." He stuck out his hand. "I'm Marc."

"Joely." Her grip was firm. "Would love to chitchat, but I need to get fuel and then up in the air. We're behind schedule and there's a storm brewing." She waited for him to climb aboard and then slammed the door behind him.

The whole time they taxied down to get gas and then as they waited in line to depart, Joely had muttered beneath her breath things he was sure he wasn't supposed to have heard. The message was clear—she was in a bad mood—so he waited until they were up in the air before he attempted to strike up a conversation.

"Think we'll beat the storm?" he asked.

Joely sighed. "We'd better. If we'd left twenty minutes later, we might not have. I'd prefer to be on the ground when those clouds break." She pointed towards the almost black clouds off in the distance.

"Will it hit the island?" He didn't anticipate experiencing his first tropical storm on his first night in Eden.

"Not where I'm staying, it won't. And that's all that matters to me. You should be wishing the same, if I were in your shoes."

Marc nodded, not really sure what she meant by that, but something told him not to ask either. He pulled out a book he'd wanted to read for ages and opened it, but he couldn't focus on the words. Instead, all he thought about was Lauren. She would be there by now. Did she get his box of chocolates? Would she understand the message?

"Oh, before I forget. Here's a message from the big guy." She reached back to hand him a folded note.

All is as planned. You've got a good friend in Paul. Don't mess it up.

Don't mess it up. What the...seriously?

"I can tell by the look on your face, you're not happy," Joely said. "Don't shoot the messenger, or in this case, the pilot. The Master has a way of—"

"Rubbing people the wrong way?" Marc interrupted her.

Her sigh was more than audible in his ears through the headphones. "He just doesn't mince his words. And he's got a special interest in your girl."

He what? "My girl. You know Lauren?"

"No. But I am the only pilot who flies the guests to

the island. Guess who was my guest earlier today?"

Marc hadn't thought of that and for some reason, the idea left him anxious.

"Was she okay? Did she come willingly? Did she seem excited, worried? Did she have any idea why she was invited?" He paused. "And what do you mean, he's got a special interest in her?" He really didn't like that part.

"Whoa, dude, enough with the questions. You'll find out soon enough. And I didn't mean it the way you think. All I know is that your buddy told him she was special and to make sure she got the royal treatment. Not many get that and if they do, there's a specific reason." Joely looked back at him and smiled.

Marc hated that smile. It seemed to be the universal look all women gave men when they were keeping a man in the dark about something. He hated it.

He turned away and looked down at the ocean and let his thoughts drift back to the last day he'd seen Lauren, exactly six years ago to the day, this weekend.

They'd met for breakfast at a local boulangerie down the street from where she was staying and lingered over their baguette and orange juice, not wanting to admit that they would soon be parting ways. Marc had loved how Lauren would reach across the table, almost without thought, and entwine her fingers with his. She was headed to Belgium, to do a chocolate tour through the small country, and then to

Germany before she headed back to Paris, but not before she stopped in Tuscany. She promised she would come back to him, to Paris, and she did. But he stood her up.

He'd been a boy in a man's body and made the worst mistake of his life. He only hoped she would understand when he tried to explain it to her.

She'd stolen his heart right from the very beginning and it wasn't until after she'd left, to complete her traveling, that the idea of a soul mate, of true love, really scared him. He knew what it meant. Knew how it would shape his life and he'd been afraid he'd have no life afterwards.

What a fool.

He would never forget the day they'd first met. There'd been an instant connection, a spark that grew quickly into a flame. She'd been standing in the line to go into the Musée d'Orsay and he'd bumped into her after he snuck in to meet his friends.

Throughout the day, they continued to run into each other at various collections until they both sat down on a bench and decided to introduce themselves. From that moment on, they'd been inseparable and Marc had fallen hard. She was his everything and he thought she felt the same way.

It had been six years, and he knew he sounded like a fool, but there was something still there, deep in his soul, for her. No one else came close to touching him the way she had. He'd tried to ignore it, played the ladies' man, was seen all over town, in the magazines, on the entertainment channels, and even Lexi had tried to set him up with her friends, but it hadn't mattered. No matter what he'd done, whom he'd dated...that connection hadn't been there.

No one could compare to Lauren.

Don't mess it up. Those words irked him. He had no plans to mess it up. He'd go on bended knee to apologize and make things right if he needed to. Everything was in place and his girl was about to get swept off her feet, one tiny toe at a time. And he was determined she wasn't going to slip away from him again. He needed her in his life, even after all this time.

CHAPTER FIVE

An hour had passed and so far, Lauren hadn't moved from the hammock strung across a corner in the more than spacious room. She was in heaven and wasn't ready to leave, no matter what the urgent knocking from her door meant.

The breeze had picked up from the open windows and with the white curtains blowing with the wind, Lauren was in her happy place. Nothing to distract her but the peace and quiet. She loved it.

Well, nothing but the constant vibration of her phone. She'd been texting Melanie since the moment she arrived.

What are you doing now?

Lauren smiled. She'd taken numerous photos of her room, the ocean, and her hammock and shown them all to her sister.

Lying in the hammock. We need one of these at home. Get out in the sun, woman!

"Ms. Summers?" There was a knock on the door but she couldn't get up. Funny how lethargic her body became once she crawled into the hammock. She really needed to get one of these at home.

The door opened and one of her Greek gods entered. She waved her hand and caught the slight shake to his head.

"I'm sorry to disturb you." Tyler came over to her and smiled down.

"I don't think I can get up." She laughed as she struggled to sit up.

Tyler reached out his hand. "There's a secret to these things, trust me. You want to keep the stool close, swing your legs out and then tilt."

Lauren reached for his hands and let him pull her out of the hammock. Out of the three brothers, Tyler was the only one who didn't wear a wedding ring. Which was perfectly fine with her. There'd been a small card resting on her bed earlier that said *The Island Knows What You Need.* Well, if the island decided she needed Tyler—then she was fine with it.

"Not sure if you noticed, but there's a storm brewing." Tyler closed all the windows in her cabin. "I need to take you to the mainland for a bit."

Lauren pulled a curtain aside and looked out. "How long will it last?" The sky was almost black and what she'd thought were soft waves hitting the posts of her cabin were actually large white caps that slammed into a barrier just out a ways. She'd grown up with storms coming off the ocean and knew this didn't look good.

"It should pass us by in a few hours. Enough time for you to have a massage and then dinner."

Her ears perked up at that. "Massage?"

"You're booked in with one of the best."

It had been ages since Lauren had last had a good massage.

I'm going for a massage!!

"And then dinner is in a little private area where you can stay relaxed. From what I hear, there's even been a special chocolate dessert prepared for you."

And there'll be chocolate at the end!

Her sister was going to be so jealous by the time her Eden vacation was over.

"Am I alone or would you be able to join me?" She smiled up at him. "I'd be more than happy to share my chocolate with you." Amazed at her own boldness, she couldn't keep the blush from showing on her cheeks, so she went into her bedroom area to grab a bag she'd found packed for her on the bed earlier. Inside were flip-flops and a book she'd wanted to read. It amazed her how well her room had been prepared, especially considering she brought no luggage with her.

When she'd first arrived, she'd found a stack of clothing on the bed and then a closet full of sundresses and cocktail dresses in her size and comfy clothing she couldn't wait to try. She wasn't sure how long she was staying, but by the look of the outfits that filled her closet, she could stay for a few weeks and not have to do laundry.

Right now, she wore cream pants that hung perfectly over her slightly rounded hips and thighs and the softest black blouse that hugged her in all the right places.

"Should I change?" she called out.

"All women are the same, aren't they? You look amazing and it's a massage." Tyler poked his head in her room and grinned. "Just bring your book and you'll be set to go."

"Are you married?"

"Why do you ask?" She liked the twinkle in his gaze.

"'Cause you sure know what to say and what not to say," Lauren teased.

Tyler laughed. "I've watched my brothers long enough with their wives to know when to shut up." Lauren grabbed one of the sundresses from the closet and stuffed it in her bag, just in case, and was about to join Tyler when she caught sight of a gold box that sat on the table beside her bed.

She didn't remember seeing that before and she

knew she wouldn't have missed this box for anything.

She knew exactly what this box was. These were Paul's signature chocolates that were no longer available. She knew they were exclusive to someone else now, but hadn't realized it was for Eden.

She grabbed the box, smiled and then snapped a photo of it.

Sure enough, there was something written on the box. Paul used to send these to her with simple messages, like *smile* or *laugh*, one word to let her know he was thinking of her. She missed those packages from him.

But the word written on this box to her didn't make sense. No one, other than her sister, knew she was here. Right?

Dream. What did that mean? Dream what? Sweet dreams? Dream of a future? What? And why?

"Are you ready?"

Lauren held up the box. "Did you bring this?"

"Are there any chocolates missing?"

Lauren opened the box and held it up for him to see.

"If they're all there, then no, I didn't bring it. You can't trust me around chocolate, I'll warn you now." He winked at her while he approached, his hand out as if to grab the box.

She hid it behind her back and shook her head. "Hands off. I won't be sharing these."

"What? You just said you'd share your chocolate with me! You can't take that back." He pouted before he shook his head. "I can't believe you got a box. Those are pretty special, from what I understand."

Lauren nodded. Special didn't adequately describe this box of chocolates.

"My friend is the chocolatier who makes them. They're one-of-a-kind and exclusive. I just didn't realize how exclusive."

"There is a small chocolate shop in the castle where there is a box of those behind lock and key. There was no price and when I asked about buying one once, I was offered a different box, one that wasn't behind that glass."

Her brows rose at that. What kind of markup did they put on them?

"Oh, don't look like that. They only meant that the Master reserves these for his special guests and makes them available to purchase extras before they leave. But...if you ever feel like sharing..."

"Hands off, buddy. I'll be savoring these babies for a long time to come." She longed to enjoy a small piece now, but decided to wait until later, when she could really savor the taste. Instead, she placed them in the small fridge in her room and heard Tyler's sigh.

"I really thought you would share at least one," he said as she turned around and then grabbed the bag off her bed.

She laughed at him.

"Not these. You'd have to be...Mr. Perfect for me to give one of these babies up."

"Give me a chance? I'd do just about anything for one of those boxes." Tyler held the door open and as he did so, a gust of wind blew in. "Come on, let's get you to the mainland while we can."

On the dock, Lauren glanced over at the other cottage that was linked to hers. There was a light on in one of the rooms and she caught the brief outline of someone as they stood at the window. She had the vague feeling that she was being watched.

"What about them?" she asked Tyler.

She caught sight of a small smile on his face. "Your neighbor? I'm sure you'll meet up with him soon enough. Sean is there with him now."

Him?

"He's alone too?"

Tyler shook his head. "He came to reconnect with his soul mate. It's a touching story, actually."

The world *soul mate* hit her hard and reminded her what this weekend was really about.

"That's nice." She held on to the bag in her hand as she followed Tyler down the wood dock and onto the beach. The warm wind blew her hair until it was all tangled and she had to shield her eyes from the sand as it kicked up.

An enclosed white golf cart waited for them at the

end of the dock. Lauren had to stifle her laughter as she watched Tyler try to climb inside. The man was a giant.

"Go ahead and laugh at my expense. Everyone else does too," Tyler muttered.

"What is it you do here?" Lauren asked as they made their way towards a small path nestled in among the bushes. It was so well hidden that she wouldn't have seen it if it weren't for being in the cart.

"A bit of this and a bit of that. Whatever the Master asks, basically."

"And how long have you and your brothers worked here?"

Tyler shrugged. "A few years now. It's not a bad gig."

Lauren thought about their wives and children. "Do you live here year round?"

He shook his head. "Some do, but not us. We have a complex on the mainland that we all share. We take shifts here, get weeks off at a time. It's not bad."

"What did you used to do before?" Lauren thought he'd probably been a bodybuilder.

"The army. All of us were. Sean just got out, a couple months ago, whereas Trev and I have been out a few years now."

"It must be nice to have your family back together. I think I would be lost without mine so close."

"Are you close with your sisters?"

Lauren nodded. "So close, we started our own company together. The youngest one does a lot of traveling, though, so I don't see her as much as I would like to."

Tyler stopped the vehicle by a set of doors and hopped out. Before Lauren could unbuckle her seatbelt, he was at her side and held his hand out for her to hold.

"You'll have to make sure you all join us next year for our triplets get-together," he said as they headed inside the main building.

Before Lauren could respond, she took a look around her and her jaw dropped. If she'd thought her little cottage was a dream come true, this place was a fairy tale. From the tall ceilings and chandeliers to the warm island pictures that lined the walls, everything about the entrance embraced her as warm and welcoming. She loved it.

If this was the side entrance, she couldn't wait to see what the main entrance looked like.

Tyler led her down a hallway and stopped at a door with an ornate sign that indicated they were entering the spa area.

"This is as far as I go." Tyler held the door open for her and waited for her to walk past him.

"Before I leave, this is for you." Tyler grabbed a box off a side table from inside the room and handed it to her. It was a beautiful gold box wrapped with a soft chocolate brown ribbon. "Don't open it until you are inside, though."

She held it up and jiggled it a little, to see if she could guess what was inside.

"Do you know what it is?" she asked him.

Tyler shook his head. "Not a clue. Whatever it is, I'm sure you'll enjoy it! The Master does love his surprises, so be warned." He gave her a smile and then closed the door behind him.

Surprises? She loved surprises, when she was the one doling them out. Today had been all about surprises and the feeling was a bit overwhelming. Within a space of six hours, she'd been whisked away to a private island she'd always dreamed of visiting, fell asleep in a hammock in the most amazing cottage she'd ever stayed at, found the best chocolates she'd ever tasted beside her bed waiting for her, and was now about to be spoiled for an evening with a massage and private dinner.

Could this evening get any better?

She smiled at him.

Well, not at him, but towards him. At least, he thought it was towards him. It could have been directed at the man who stood beside her, but he preferred to think the smile was meant for him.

Except, she didn't know he was there.

He itched to send a text to Paul, to ask for his advice on what to do next, but every time he went to send his message, he would delete it instead. He needed to man up and just do what needed to be done, follow his plan and not freak out. But when he saw her there, steps away from him...everything fell to pieces.

His plan. His goal. His heart.

After six long years of only remembering her smile, to see it again...she took his breath away. He knew he was being sappy, but damn it, he didn't care.

"You're a lucky man," Sean said.

Sean had met him at the dock earlier when he'd landed and was here to bring him inland, thanks to the storm.

"I hope so," Marc said.

"Everything is all set for tonight. She's on her way to a massage and then will meet you for dinner." Sean slapped him on the back and Marc winced from the impact. Compared to Sean, Marc was a bean pole. His six-foot muscular frame had nothing on Sean, or his brothers, from what he'd seen earlier.

"Thanks for doing that," Marc said.

"Dude, I didn't do anything. I'm just the messenger here." Sean stood by the front door. "And we need to leave. I really don't want to get caught when the rain hits."

Marc followed him out the front door and down the dock.

"Where are we headed, anyways?" he asked.

"It's tacky games night tonight and I figured you needed something to keep your mind off the time until dinner."

"Games night?"

Sean nodded. "It's fun and guests usually love it. Tonight it's staff against guests and winners get a fondue party. I'm under strict orders to make sure we win, too."

The look on Sean's face made him laugh. "Strict orders? From who?"

"My pregnant wife. She's been craving chocolate fondue for the past couple days now."

Marc climbed into the golf cart that waited at the end of the dock. He was amazed at how quickly the wind had picked up.

"I thought Joely had said the storm shouldn't hit the island?" Marc complained. He'd hoped to have dinner outside on the dock between both his and Lauren's cottage. There was a nice little area behind them but the storm had kiboshed that idea.

Sean shrugged. "Looks like it's only hitting this side, which is odd since it's not a large island. But...you never know what will happen here."

"What does that mean?" He'd heard that saying a few times now, or something similar.

"The island knows what you need. Don't you feel it? The way it pulses around you? Almost like it's alive."

Marc raised his brows at that. Alive? The island? It was a landmass stuck in the middle of a large body of water. How would it know what he wanted or even needed?

"Don't doubt, man. Don't doubt. I've seen things happen here that wouldn't—couldn't—happen anywhere else. Trust me. The storm is here for a reason."

"It had better be a good one. I had plans that involved dinner and watching the sunset right on that dock behind us." Marc scoffed.

Sean only shook his head. "If tonight doesn't work out better than you originally planned, I'll..."

"Buy me a drink?" Marc guessed.

Sean chuckled. "Sure, if that works." He pulled up to a side entrance of the massive castle and parked the cart. "We'll go in this way, a lot faster and less chance of running into a certain somebody too early." He winked at Marc before he led the way.

His body was a bundle of nerves, but he attempted to keep his cool. It was difficult, though. In a little over an hour, he'd be face to face with Lauren, the girl his heart couldn't let go.

He followed Sean down a hallway and out into a sheltered courtyard, and couldn't get over the amount of people there. For some reason, he'd been under the impression the island wasn't that busy this weekend but he should have known better.

"Crazy, right? With the storm, everyone is coming up to the mainland. Give it another hour or so and you won't be able to grab a seat." Sean led him over to a large table where his other brother and two women—he assumed the wives—all sat.

"Marc, this is Trev, and Tyler..." he glanced around and then shrugged, "will be here shortly."

"He's with Lauren still," Trevor said. He stuck his hand out to Marc. "Good to meet you.

Marc looked from Sean to Trevor and back to Sean and caught the faint look of disapproval in Sean's gaze.

"You've only got a little over an hour, so what do you say we get the games started?" Sean rubbed his hands together and looked about the room. "Ping-pong. Let's go!"

Marc watched as Sean took off and shook his head. Ping-pong? Really?

"Be warned, he's a fanatic when it comes to that ball and paddle," Trevor said.

"How fanatic?" A man and his sport was never to be trifled with. Personally, he preferred rugby.

"Won state championship in high school and got a team started while stationed overseas a few years ago. The group is still going strong."

Marc groaned. "What's with guys and little balls? Give me a big one any day." The moment he said it, he knew it came out wrong. "Rugby, dude. Rugby."

Trevor slapped him on the back before he pushed him along to follow after Sean.

Marc was itching to do anything other than play Ping-pong, but it would probably be a good way to vent some steam, release some energy and waste time until after Lauren's massage.

He checked over his shoulder to see whether Tyler had come in but he didn't see the guy yet. Which worried him. They all knew the reason she was here, right? For him? Which meant, hands off, right?

But the thing was...Lauren didn't know that. A sinking feeling hit him then. What if he were too late?

Maybe the massage had been a bad idea. Maybe he should have been the one to meet her when she first arrived? What had he been thinking? Why had he let Lexi and Paul talk him into spoiling her for a bit before he revealed himself?

How could he have been so stupid?

CHAPTER SIX

She couldn't move. She was literally glued to the bed and there was no way on God's green earth she was moving from this spot.

The massage therapist had golden hands and knew all the right spots to work. She couldn't believe how tense and tight she'd been and how amazing she felt right now. She tried to move her legs to the side but they were loose jelly. A giggle escaped before she could stop it.

Maybe she shouldn't have had that extra glass of wine before the massage? She peeked at her fingers and smiled. That wine had been worth it because it meant she now had the prettiest shade of coral pink on both her fingers and toes.

"Do you need some help, ma'am?" There was a

knock on the door.

"I can't seem to get up," Lauren called out. She giggled again. She knew how silly she must look but she didn't care.

"This has been the best day of my life in a long, long time." She smiled up at her miracle worker, who only shook her head, helped to adjust the sheet around her body and then pulled her up to a sitting position.

"Make sure you hydrate a lot before bed and tomorrow will be just as good."

"Water. Right. I'm sorry we went over the allotted time." Her pretty nails were worth it, though.

"Don't you worry about it. You are my last client of the day and honestly, probably my most fun." Her miracle worker smiled before she stepped back out into the hallway. "Oh, I placed some warmed up towels outside the shower doors for you. Enjoy your shower."

Lauren sat there, hunched over, not really wanting to move any more than she had to, but then her stomach grumbled and she knew if she didn't eat something soon, she'd pay for it later. The small plate of cheese she'd munched on earlier with her wine really hadn't cut it and considering she hadn't had much to eat all day...no wonder the wine went straight to her head.

She hopped off the bed and the sheet pooled at her feet before she headed into the shower just off the room. The hot water rained down over her relaxed muscles. She leaned up against the tiled walls and let out a long breath. How was she supposed to get out of here and make it to dinner?

It took awhile, but she managed to crawl her way out of the shower and get dressed. She was thankful that the summer dress she'd thrown in to the bag fit her properly. How they managed to find her clothes that fit her hourglass figure was beyond her. She normally had a hard enough time trying to find something to fit her hips and thighs while accommodating her larger than preferred chest.

"I hear you're all done." Tyler's voice was on the other side of the door and Lauren's stomach flip-flopped at his voice. She stuck her feet in her sandals, grabbed her bag and opened the door, a huge smile on her face.

"That was amazing." She leaned against the wall.

"You look amazing," was all Tyler said. He held out his arm and she reached for it. "Ready for dinner?"

Her stomach growled loud enough for him to hear.

"I'll take that as a yes."

"I've been looking forward to this meal since you mentioned it." The only question, in her mind, was whether she would be eating alone or with a certain muscular Greek god that could take her mind off what this whole weekend was about.

She preferred option two. She didn't want to think about Marc. Not anymore. It was time to let him go, time to move past the hope she harbored deep inside.

Who was she kidding? Despite the sweet smiles, and the feel of his muscular arms beneath her hand, she'd trade this hunk for Marc any day. If the island really knew what she needed, it would have brought Marc to her.

"Why the frown?" Tyler stopped outside a set of white French doors. A warm glow emanated from behind the soft white curtains that covered the glass on the other side.

She shrugged. "No reason, other than this dinner signifies the end to an amazing day."

"What if it wasn't the end, but rather the beginning to something you've always dreamed about?"

Lauren just looked at him, not bothering to respond.

"The island knows what you want and need..."

She laughed. "Then the island should know I'm wanting something chocolate for dessert and then a warm breeze while I lay in the hammock tonight."

"Just wait and see." He leaned down and placed a soft kiss on her cheek. "Leave your heart open, okay?"

Puzzled, Lauren watched Tyler as he walked away from her. She was really going to have dinner by herself, on this island where supposedly her dreams were to come true? Really? Whoever planned this day for her forgot one tiny tidbit of information. She hated eating alone. There was nothing worse than being alone at a table surrounded by couples who whispered sweet promises to each other.

She had half a mind to walk away and find her own way down to her cottage for the night when she remembered the promise of chocolate. And the fact she wasn't sure how to navigate the maze Tyler had walked her into.

With a sigh, she turned the knob on the door and pushed it open.

The warm glow in the room surrounded her, the soft music that played danced around her but it was the sight in front of her, or rather the person, that made her already weak knees give out until she crumpled to the floor in a heap.

Marc was here. He couldn't be. That couldn't be him. Could it?

Whomever it was, he rushed over to her and knelt down.

Neither one said anything. Lauren couldn't. Her mouth had gone dry and all she could think was why. Why?

"Hello, beautiful," Marc said to her.

Marc. It was really him. She would know his voice anywhere, because it still whispered to her in the middle of the night, even now, after six years of believing she wasn't enough for him.

She smiled and raised her hand to gently stroke his cheek. It was really him.

"I've missed you," Lauren whispered. She swallowed past the lump in her throat and then struggled to get up.

With her hands firmly enclosed in Marc's, he helped her up off the ground and they both stood there, their hands clasped, small smiles on their faces as they stared at each other.

"I take everything back that I thought about this island. I love it," Lauren said.

Marc's eyes lit up and he pulled her close. "I can't believe you're here. Really here." His gaze traveled over her face and she loved the way he appeared to be memorizing everything about her.

It had been six years. She wasn't as young, or as skinny as she had been back then. There were a few wrinkles at the corner of her eyes and her skin didn't glow like it used to. Did he notice?

"I..." they both said at the same time, stopped and then said it again before they laughed.

"You go," Lauren said.

Marc shook his head. "No, you."

They were at a stalemate and Lauren loved it. Happiness flooded her soul and she couldn't believe he was here, in the flesh. That it was his skin touching hers, his presence that filled her up...him.

Her hungry stomach beat them both as it growled

loud enough to fill the room. Lauren winced before she looked behind Marc at the table and noticed the basket of bread there.

"Are you here to have dinner with me?" What a silly question, and yet...she was afraid to take anything for granted right now. It felt like a dream come true, having him here. But not all dreams ended with a happy ending.

"I thought that would be a nice way to end your day, if that's okay?"

She felt a bit tongue-tied. What was she to say? Ask him how he'd been? Why he'd been silent for six years? Why he stood her up and never contacted her? Why he was here, now?

"I'd love that," was all she said.

Marc pulled out a chair for her and she caught the brief scent of his aftershave. Still smelled the same. When he sat beside her, there was a brief lull between them that carried a sense of awkwardness.

She watched him, as he buttered his bread, poured their wine and did anything else at the table that would normally be considered mundane. She memorized the way he moved, the way he held his knife, cocked his head and even smiled at her. Everything she would need to get her through the next six years.

As much as this seemed like a dream come true, even she knew princesses woke up from their slumber.

If they'd ended right there and then, with things being on the surface between them, she could have gone back to her room in a state of bliss, excited about what tomorrow would bring.

But then Marc had to ruin it.

"I couldn't believe it when Lexi showed me a photo of the two of you on the beach."

Lauren almost sputtered the wine she'd just sipped and ended up coughing instead.

"You know Lexi?" she managed to squeak out after her extreme coughing fit.

She asked the question again, despite his nod. It wasn't possible. How could he know her best friend? How?

"I've known her for a few years now. Since she started to date Paul."

Her heart sunk. He knew both her best friends. How, in God's green earth, could they have gone six years and never once mentioned Marc to her?

"They never mentioned me before?"

He shook his head and then shrugged. His posture was suddenly rigid and he pulled away from her a bit.

It was only a slight tilt, but it spoke volumes.

"I don't understand. They're my best friends." Marc heard the solid emphasis on *my*. "Lauren and I went to school together, and I met Paul during my trip to Europe, after..."

Marc nodded. "After you left me in Paris. I know.

He told me all about it."

"Paul told you...when? When did he tell you all about it?"

"Last week."

"Last..." He'd only found out about her last week? She'd talked to Lexi a few times during the week, and there'd been a flurry of text messages between her and Paul yesterday over the wedding cake he was making for her client.

Marc nodded, a somber look in his eyes. "I wish I had known years ago...so close and yet, so far apart."

Lauren let out a haggard breath and felt as if everything inside her was being wrenched apart. Lexi and Paul had been in her life forever. How could Marc's name never come up? How? She shook her head and rubbed her neck as she racked her brain to remember whether he'd ever been mentioned. He must have.

"What is Paul to you?" Maybe they were just passing friends. That would explain it. And she'd never really told Lexi about Marc, never had to. They both nursed their broken hearts in private, knowing there'd been a connection between them but never needing to explore the reason behind it.

"He's my best friend and business partner."

Her head whipped up. "What?" She pushed aside her half-eaten dinner and reached for her glass of wine.

"I know. How have we never crossed paths before? How?" He shook his head but then reached his hand over to touch hers.

She moved hers away.

She wasn't sure how to react, how to respond, or even what to do. This was crazy. Crazy.

There had to be something he wasn't telling her. Something he was hiding from her. She pushed her chair back and guzzled her wine, not taking the time to savor it as it slid down her throat.

"I'm sorry. I mourned you. Mourned you for six years. I thought I'd lost you forever...why didn't you come and meet me?" She reached for the wine bottle; she poured the liquid into her glass and then gulped it back again.

Did she really want to know the answer? Wasn't it better to live in her dream world, with all the scenarios she'd built up for herself?

"I mean, I know your parents were ill," she stared down at her wine and swirled it in the cup, "so I just assumed something happened and that's why you never showed up." She lifted her gaze but he stared down at the table. That didn't look good.

She needed to get drunk and fast. Maybe then her mind would be able to process this and stop her heart from breaking apart again.

"You never called me. Never said goodbye." She hiccupped. She wanted to die from embarrassment.

This was her tell, or so her sisters said, for when she was upset. "Never explained why," hiccup, "you weren't there when I," hiccup, "returned."

All the tears she'd cried in secret, all the whispered longings, the questions she'd never been able to share with anyone poured out of her and the only thing she now felt was relief.

Relief to let it all out.

"I've loved you forever." She took a deep breath, calmer now. "I loved you until there was nothing left inside me, and you didn't care. You tossed me aside, like I wasn't worth anything, and moved on." She wiped at the tears before she pushed her chair back even farther. Her legs wobbled as she stood there and she was suddenly nervous that she'd fall down again, at his feet.

Oh God. She wanted him to deny it, to give her an explanation that made perfect sense, one she could easily forgive and understand. Like his mom was on her deathbed, or an emergency had come up and he'd tried to get there but... All he did was sit there, his gaze downward, as if he were too embarrassed by her reactions.

"I'm sorry," he finally said.

She waited for something else, for an explanation, but he just sat there. And the longer he sat there, the more her ire picked up until she wasn't embarrassed but rather angry with him and his lack of response.

"I'm sorry? That's all you have to say?"

He finally looked up then and in that moment, she knew, no matter what he said, she would rather have lived with not knowing.

"We were just kids."

Lauren took another drink of her wine and sputtered at that.

"Just kids? It was only six years ago, Marc. I'm almost thirty now. I think I was more than *just a kid.*" If he dared to use that as an excuse...

"I'm sorry. That came out wrong." Marc sighed and ran his fingers through his hair. She could tell he was nervous.

"I made a mistake. One I've regretted every day since."

She swallowed hard. She wanted to stop him, to tell him to stop, but she couldn't. She knew, though, that she would hate everything he was about to tell her. Everything she'd worried about but never wanted to admit.

"You never came, did you?" she said.

He shook his head. "I couldn't."

She almost sighed with relief. He didn't come because his mother was sick. That had to be it.

"I was scared."

"Scared of what?"

"Of our future." He stared at her, a plea in his gaze, and she tried so hard to be understanding.

"What about the stories you told me of your parents? How they were soul mates and how you wanted a love like that. How we could have a love like that. Did you lie to me?"

Marc reached out to her but she stepped out of his reach.

"I didn't lie. But once you were gone, reality sunk in and I...I wasn't ready. Lauren, I wasn't ready for what love really meant."

That hit her in the gut, hard. "What did you think it meant? That it would ruin your life?" By the look on his face, that's exactly what he'd thought.

After six years of wondering why he never showed up, never contacted her...now she knew and it wasn't what her dreams had been made of.

"Reality sucks, sometimes," she whispered. "I've held you up to a high standard. I loved you. *Loved* you. But I never really knew you, did I?" Her nostrils flared as she struggled not to cry. She needed to get out of here, away from him. But he stepped towards her and reached out. She smacked his hand away, wishing it had been his face or chest she'd hit instead. "Leave me alone."

She rushed through the door, not caring that she'd just left her heart broken on the floor behind her, and ran down the hallway. She almost tripped over Tyler, who stood there at the end.

"Whoa, slow down." Tyler's grip on her arms

soothed her. She sank into him and let the feel of his arms around her comfort her.

"Can you take me back, please." Her voice was muffled against his shirt.

"Lauren." Marc called her name.

She raised her head and looked up at Tyler. "Please?" she begged.

She read the concern in his gaze and breathed a sigh of relief at his nod. He turned them both and went down a short hallway until they exited through a door, down another hallway and then out into the night.

Lauren tilted her head back as a warm breeze wrapped itself around her.

"Looks like the storm ended, just in time," Tyler said. He led her to a cart, helped her in and then drove down a pathway. Lauren had no idea where they were but she knew they were headed towards the water. The sound of the surf crashing upon the sand welcomed her as they pulled up to the wood deck.

Without a word, Tyler helped her out of the cart and walked with her up to the cottage. The lights were on, candles aflame all around the room and the tears welled up again.

"Are you going to be okay?" Tyler asked.

She nodded, not trusting herself to speak before she shook her head. No, she wasn't going to be okay. She was confused. More than confused. Hurt and even a little angry, but she wasn't sure who to blame.

"Do you...would you like some company?" Tyler asked her.

Lauren let out a small laugh, which turned into a cry. She sat down on the couch and sobbed into her hands. Tyler joined her and pulled her into his arms, giving her a refuge while she continued to cry.

Eventually she sat up and patted at his now wet chest. She took the tissue he held out to her and wiped her eyes and nose. She wasn't a pretty crier; she knew her face would be all blotchy, her nose swollen and her eyes bright red, so she attempted to hide her face from him.

Tyler scooted to the edge of the couch and briefly touched her knee. "How about some chocolate?" he asked.

She laughed, and when she realized it sounded like a croak, she laughed again.

"I never did get dessert," she said.

His eyes widened. "We need to fix that then. Why don't you go have a hot bath and relax and I'll make sure you get some of that dessert I heard was being made for you tonight. Okay?"

She pulled her knees up to her chest and nodded.

"Are you going to be okay?" He asked.

She attempted a small smile. "I'll be fine after that chocolate." Chocolate was always the answer, no matter the situation.

"I'll come by in the morning and take you for

breakfast, okay?"

"You won't be back?" The minute she asked, she knew she'd been a fool. Of course he wouldn't be. He wasn't the reason she was here and it wasn't fair of her to lean on him right now.

"Forget it—silly question." She let out a long sigh. "See you tomorrow." She rubbed her face, sniffled a bit and rested her head back on the couch while Tyler left.

Now what? What was she supposed to do? Marc was here. HERE. She'd envisioned this night for years, working through scenarios if she ever met him again. Never had she thought of this one.

She jumped up from the couch and headed into the bedroom, where her phone rested on the nightstand. She picked it up and checked to ensure there was a signal.

Tell me you didn't know. She texted Lexi.

While she waited for a response, she headed into the bathroom where a large, two-person claw tub sat, and started the water. A long soak was exactly what she needed right now.

Thirty minutes later, her phone buzzed.

Give him a chance, Lexi texted back.

Lauren couldn't believe what she read. Lexi had known. She'd known and not said anything.

Give him a chance? Are you kidding me? How could you? You should have told me. Given me a heads-up at least.

I'm sorry.

So am I. Lauren had no idea what to do now.

He loves you.

Lauren snorted at that. *So much, that he stood me up six years ago and never looked back.*

Let him explain. Please.

Explain? What could he possibly say?

No. She thought she'd been in love with a man, but all she'd been in love with was a memory. And that hurt more than anything else.

How was she supposed to deal with that?

CHAPTER SEVEN

He'd paced his cottage all night and waited for the lights in her room to go out. It had taken everything inside him to leave her alone, to not go to her and try to explain.

Last night had been a disaster.

He'd almost been out the door when the light in her room finally went out. He could have kicked himself for chickening out, for not manning up and going after her.

What had he been thinking?

He'd finally sent Paul a text and Lexi her own separate one and realized what an ass he'd been. Give her time, was their advice. But he knew better. He'd known better. She'd already had six years—why had he allowed another minute to go by? Why?

He checked the time and hoped he'd given her more than enough time to get up and get dressed. He wasn't willing to waste another minute without her by his side. He didn't care whether she was angry or sad or...no, he lied. He did care. He cared more than he thought possible.

Watching her run from him last night just about killed him. But to see her in another man's arms destroyed him.

He reached for the bag she'd left behind last night and left his small cottage. The moment he stepped outside, the bright glare from the sun blinded him and despite lowering his sunglasses, it took a few seconds for him to see that he wasn't alone on the deck.

Lauren was there, outside his door. Waiting for him.

"Hi, neighbor," she said. Her voice was low, a bit hesitant but it warmed him like the sun couldn't.

He swallowed.

"Hi, back." Hi back? That's what he said? Honestly? He joined her at the railing, where she was half leaning, and handed her the bag in his hands.

"Thanks." She set the bag down and leaned her elbows on the wood rail to stare out over the ocean.

He couldn't take his gaze off her. She was beautiful. Her dark brown hair shimmered in the sunlight; the length of it rested on her shoulders and curled down around the tops of her arms. She wore a beautiful white sundress with soft pink sandals and her skin glowed.

She was a goddess and he so much wanted to kiss her.

He turned and stared out over the water as well, hoping to find something there to hold his attention but there was nothing. Just...water. So he turned back to her, not caring if she noticed.

"Have you had breakfast?" he asked. They could talk about why she took off last night later. Right now, all he wanted was to spend time with her. He realized last night that he needed to try a different tactic with her.

Six years ago, there had been an instant connection. He needed to prove to her that it was still there. He'd seen it last night between them before everything had fallen apart. He planned to go slow, to show her that he was still the same guy she'd fallen in love with in Paris.

"Not yet. I was...I was going to see if you wanted to join me?" A brief smile kissed her lips and his heart swelled.

"Funny, I was about to do the same. I figured if this island is as magical as it's made out to be, we should be able to find a proper croissant or baguette somewhere, right?"

Lauren groaned. "I would kill for a Parisian baguette right about now. American bread just isn't the same."

His brow lifted. "Is that right? Well then, let's go find one, shall we?" He held out his hand and caught the way she hesitated before she reached out and placed her hand in his.

"We need to talk—" she began but he cut her off.

"Breakfast first. We can talk about last night later. There's no rush, okay?" He needed her relaxed, not all tense and apprehensive.

"Okay." Her shoulders relaxed and when she took in a deep breath and then let it out, he knew there was a chance.

"Let me just put this bag back inside." She glanced down inside the bag and hesitated. "I forgot about this." She pulled out a box with a brown colored bow and held it up. "Tyler gave this to me last night and I was going to open it after my massage."

Marc stilled...he knew what was in the box and he wasn't sure if he wanted her to open it right now.

"Oh, I wonder if it's more chocolates." She bit her lip as she played with the brown ribbon. "Although, more chocolates would be a bit of a letdown, especially after getting Paul's gold boxed chocolates."

"You got one of those?" Who would have given them to her? Paul? The guy who owned the island? What was written on it?

Her face lit up. "I did. And I'm not sharing." Her eyes twinkled and he was reminded about her love for chocolate. "Unless...any way you could convince Paul to send me more of those boxes?"

Marc took his time answering that. His friendship with Paul was the reason she took off last night.

"I can't even get these." He decided to be honest.

She scrunched up her nose at that but when her stomach grumbled, she placed the box back in the bag. "I'll worry about this after breakfast."

Marc waited for her to open her cottage door and slip the bag inside.

"How did you know where I was staying?" he asked.

She lifted her shoulder. "I had a hunch after something Tyler said last night."

"What was that?"

She looked as if she were about to answer but then stopped. There was something in her gaze, mischievous but happy. Satisfied even. He knew he could prod but didn't want to. She'd tell him eventually. He hoped.

They walked down the boardwalk and made their way along the beach. More buildings were off in the distance. Not in a rush, Marc made sure his pace was slow to match Lauren's. He asked her a few questions about her flight to the island and whether she'd done any exploring so far.

"I thought maybe today, I would. There was a pamphlet in the room detailing today's activities. Did you know there is a sunken ship somewhere close by?" Lauren said.

"Do you snorkel?" He hoped she said no.

"I love it. You?"

As much as he hated to admit it, he shook his head and gazed out at the water. "I can't swim."

He'd only admitted that to a few people. He loved the beach, the feel of the sand beneath his feet and thoroughly enjoyed visiting the coast during the weekend with Paul and playing a round of beach volleyball. But other than playing around in the water close to the shoreline in France, he never went any farther than his chest.

Paul knew he couldn't swim and made fun of him on a constant basis. Only Lexi knew why.

He expected to see pity or sadness in Lauren's gaze but what he didn't expect was for her to reach out and touch him. She laid her hand on his arm and squeezed.

"Then snorkling is out of the question."

He smiled down at her, thankful for her understanding. That's when it hit him, a memory from when they'd first met. She'd wanted to go to the top of the Eiffel Tower and had tried to coax him into going up with her. When he'd finally confessed his fear of heights, going to the top of the tower wasn't a goal for her anymore. Just like that. No pouting, no guilt trips. Just acceptance.

Even then she'd been an angel.

They rounded a corner and came upon what looked like a beach cafe, complete with outdoor tables and umbrellas. To the side was a lounge area with wicker furniture all situated so you could sit and watch the water.

"Let's stop here," Lauren said. She headed to a table, sat down, leaned back and smiled with contentment. She looked happy, which made him happy. And sappy.

He couldn't believe how sappy he felt. Paul would rib him for sure.

"Do you think they'll have baguettes and hand-squeezed orange juice?" she asked him as he sat down beside her.

"If the island is as magical as I'm told it is, they should."

"Should we test it?" Her eyes twinkled.

"How?" He was game.

"What's something you've craved for breakfast but can never find?"

Marc thought about that. Since his parents' passing, he'd missed his mom's shirred eggs. She would add homegrown herbs from her window box, some mushroom and ham and serve it for breakfast on the weekends.

"It would be sweet if they had oeuf cocotte." He wondered whether she would know what that meant.

She cocked her head and stared up at him. "That

means shirred egg, right?"

"Oui. Très bon."

He felt as if he'd just won a lifetime of eggs from the way she smiled up at him.

"The last time Jess came home from one of her trips to France, she only spoke French to us for a month." She shook her head.

"She did that because..."

Lauren groaned. "She thought it would add a new component to our company if we could speak in different languages. As much as I hated her for it at the time, it's worked to our advantage over and over. We now all take classes in different languages."

"How many languages can you speak?"

"Not as many as you'd think. French and a bit of German. That's it. I'm to start a new class next month to improve my German. It's a nine-week course and I promised myself if I got an A, then I would plan a trip there."

"Impressive. German's an easy language to learn. It's been awhile since I was last there."

She narrowed her gaze at him. "Don't tell me you're fluent."

His reply was to shrug his shoulder.

"Marc." She sighed. "Is there anything you can't do?"

"I can't speak Korean. Or Japanese. Or Chinese. Or snorkel."

"True. Okay, I can handle that. So you're not perfect. Good to know." Her cheeks blushed and she lowered her gaze to the table.

Just then, someone Marc only assumed was the waiter came out and handed them menus. The kid looked like someone who should be on a surf board and not serving tables.

"Question," Marc asked the guy. "Do you have fresh baguettes, fresh squeezed orange juice and—"

"It's all in the menu, dude."

"Excuse me?" Lauren said. She sat up in her chair and frowned.

"I'm just filling in. I work in the surf shop but somethin's going on over at the mainland and I was sent here." The kid shrugged and crossed his arms.

"Do you know what?" Marc asked.

"Nope."

"Okay then." Marc looked over the menu and found exactly what he'd been hoping to find.

"I'll have the Parisian special number five."

"And I'll have the number two," Lauren said.

Marc glanced over down to see what Lauren had ordered and smiled. Two hard boiled eggs, half a baguette with homemade jam, and freshly squeezed orange juice.

Exactly what she'd wanted.

They handed the kid their menus.

"So there may be a little bit of magic after all,"

Lauren said.

"We'll see if the eggs are as good as my mom's." Marc winked at her.

"How are your parents?"

Marc glanced away. He stared out into the ocean and watched the way the waves gently rolled onto the shore and thought about his mom and how she'd loved the trips to the ocean when he was a child.

"They passed away about a year ago," he said.

"Both of them?"

He nodded and swallowed, hard. "Mom passed away first. She just died in her sleep one night. Dad..." He swallowed again and shifted in his seat. "Dad went shortly after. I think it was too much for him, being alone after so long. He told me his place was with my mom, that he was only half the man he used to be and a few days later, he was gone."

Lauren leaned forward and grabbed his hand. "I'm so sorry."

Marc nodded but didn't say anything. He still choked up when he thought of it. Of them. Of their love. It was because of his parents that he believed in soul mates and true love and love at first sight. Because he knew it was real.

"They loved each other with a passion I've never seen before. I...I can only hope to love as hard as my father did. Mom was his life." He smiled and stared down into Lauren's eyes. "She was his heart and soul, and he knew it from the moment they first met." He didn't look away, just prayed that she understood what he tried to say.

"I think I would be lost without my parents. I know how important they were to you. I'm sorry."

The silence grew between them at that.

Their server came back out with some cups and a canister of coffee. He set it down and attempted to pour until Lauren reached out and helped him. She steadied the coffee cups and took the cream and sugar from his tray and set it down on the table.

"Sorry," the guy mumbled beneath his breath before he headed back into the cafe.

"Poor kid." Lauren poured him a cup of coffee before she filled her own cup. Marc drank his black but if his memory was right, Lauren needed both sugar and cream in hers.

"Black?" he said, a bit surprised.

She brought the cup up close to her mouth and inhaled. "It took me a bit, but it was either drink coffee black or give up chocolate."

"What?"

"A bet between me and Melanie. I lost."

"Do I even dare to ask?" From the look on her face, she didn't seem too bothered to have lost.

She laughed, took a sip of her coffee and set it down.

"It was silly. She said I couldn't go a week without

chocolate and I said I could do a month."

"You? Give up chocolate? Even I would know that was crazy."

She shrugged. "I don't like being so predictable. But, yeah, kind of silly." She leaned back and sighed. "I've kind of grown to enjoy the taste of coffee now that it's not covered up in cream.

"I wish they were here." Lauren cleared her throat and leaned forward. "Melanie and I have had a long fascination with Eden and we've often fantasized what it would be like here. She would love it. The calmness, how serene it is. Although...it might be too tame for her." There was a faraway look in her gaze and for a moment he felt jealous of her relationship with her sisters. He wanted her focus to be on the here and now, on him.

"Is it for you?" He wanted her to walk away from this with a heart full of memories, and hopefully, love. For him.

"Too tame?" When he nodded, she shook her head. "Not at all. This is exactly what I always dreamed of. The quiet. Listening to the waves, knowing there was no schedule, no appointments, no clients I needed to take care of."

"You take care of a lot of people in your life, don't you?"

She nodded. "That's my job. Bella Dia is...well, it's my life. We all have a role in the company, my sisters and I, but mine is exactly that—taking care of things, of our clients. Ensuring their every need is met. Jessica finds all the amazing locations, Melanie takes care of the practicalities, and I...I take care of my clients." Her shoulders slumped and she leaned back in her chair. For a moment, Marc caught the look of exhaustion on her face and he heard the words she didn't say.

"But who takes care of you?" He couldn't help himself. He touched her hand and threaded his fingers through hers.

"I don't really need to be taken care of. I'm okay."

Marc just raised his brows. Even he heard the lackluster in her voice. She needed to be taken care of and he needed to be the one to do it. He felt it, deep inside.

"Will you let me?" He hadn't meant to ask her. Hadn't meant to say the words out loud. But he did and now his world rested on her answer.

"Don't answer that." He wasn't sure he could handle knowing. Not yet. It was too early, too soon. There was more to be done, more that he needed to do, to show. There was something there between them, something that went beyond physical attraction, although he could see it in the way she subconsciously leaned towards him while they walked side by side, and even now, how she was angled towards him. He knew body language and he could read hers loud and clear.

There was more between them, though. It was in the silence, the peace. He just needed her to realize it, to believe in it. To believe in him and what they have.

He needed to prove to her that they had more than just a memory of love.

CHAPTER EIGHT

Would she let him? Her heart basically melted the moment he asked. She almost said yes before he stopped her.

He stopped her. Why? Why would he do that? Was he unsure? Did he regret asking?

All morning, all she'd wanted to do was lean into him and wrap her arms around his waist and feel him, his strength. She wanted to have the feel of his arms around her and to know it wasn't all in her memory.

And he'd stopped her. Maybe it was for the best.

Last night, she'd gone to bed with a plan. She'd been pissed. Well, more than a little pissed. But once she calmed down and really thought about what he'd said...she couldn't fault him for being scared six years ago. She did blame him for how he reacted—standing her up was not okay, but if he asked her to forgive him, she would. It was in the past.

She'd realized last night that she had a choice. It was obvious he wanted a second chance, so the ball was in her court. She'd held on to the memory of them for so long...was she willing to give it up all because he made a mistake? Her pride said yes...that he wasn't worth her heart, but her heart...her heart said differently.

But today was a new day. A new chance. And she was going to do everything she could to give whatever they had between them that chance.

She'd thought he wanted the same, except now it didn't sound as if he was too sure.

They ate their breakfast in silence. Every time she'd wanted to say something, she stopped herself.

What could she say?

Yes, there was a connection between them. The past six years seemed to just melt away but that didn't negate the fact that for years he'd given up on them.

Something neither one had the courage to bring up, apparently.

"Answer me one question." She decided to dare it. To bring it up and see what he had to say.

"Anything."

"Why couldn't you tell me how you felt? Why did you think standing me up and then remaining silent for six years was the right thing to do? After all, you had my information."

The look on Marc's face gave her pause. As if he couldn't believe she asked him that.

"You didn't leave me your contacts. I went back, a few days afterwards, hoping maybe you'd left a message, but there'd been nothing. I blamed myself. You were probably mad at me for not showing up, for not being there." His voice remained calm, at ease, but the way the veins in his neck stood out and how tight he gripped his fork...he was anything but calm.

"I was," she admitted. She leaned forward and rested her elbow on the table. "My parents had been in a car accident and I couldn't stay. I wanted to. I thought about going back the next morning to see if maybe you'd been held up, but I couldn't. So I left them a letter to give to you."

"A letter?"

She nodded.

"You left me a letter."

"Did you not get it?" There was a sick twist in her gut and she needed to move, to walk, to be anywhere but in this chair. She pushed it back and stood.

"Where are you going?" Marc wiped his mouth with the napkin and stood.

Lauren's chest was tight and she knew she was about to have one of her classic panic attacks when things were out of her control.

"I need to walk." She struggled to breathe in deep.

"I just need to walk." She left him standing there and took off, almost running until she was down by the water. She took off her sandals and looked back to see that Marc spoke with the waiter.

She felt bad for leaving him like that but she had no choice.

Her thoughts went round and round, like one of those horses on a merry-go-round. She left him a letter. He never wrote her. Never contacted her. But then, maybe he didn't get it. For years, she'd thought that, wondered that...but the owner had promised her Marc would get it.

Promised her.

He'd stood her up but then he'd gone back...that said something. That told her that he'd been able to move past his fear...but it had still been too late. Inside, she was unsettled. She wasn't sure how she was supposed to feel: Angry? Sad? Confused? All of those?

The water lapped the shoreline and caressed her toes. It was warm and felt refreshing, so she stepped farther in until her ankles were submerged. She stood there and watched the way the sun danced along the water, sparkling like diamonds, and hugged herself as Marc stood at her side.

"It almost feels like we were doomed from the start, doesn't it?"

"No, love. Not doomed. We just weren't ready."

She shook her head. "The owner promised me you'd get the letter. She promised. I always wondered...thought that maybe you hadn't gotten it, but then I would remember the way you'd talk with the owner, how friendly you were and that she was a friend of your parents."

She turned to him and when she caught the look in his eyes, she knew...

"But you never got it. She never gave it to you, because..."

He turned to her and placed his hands on her shoulders. "Because she knew my mother wouldn't understand my being in love with a foreigner." The way he said it, so sad and forlorn, told her more than she probably wanted to know.

She sighed and in that release of breath, she let out everything that she'd kept bottled up inside her. All the pain of the past six years, of feeling unloved, neglected, unworthy. The sadness of knowing that what they had wasn't real. The heaviness of wondering whether she'd done something, anything, to cause his silence.

"And if you'd gotten the letter...would you have contacted me? Or would you have left things alone and been a good French boy who listened to his mother? Would you have kept running?"

"I would have written you. Emailed you. I would have begged for your forgiveness for not being there and for being so foolish. And then I would have done anything and everything to make it work."

She closed her eyes at his words.

"But in the end, we both would have known it couldn't have."

"Could you have left your parents?"

She shook her head. "The accident was rough. Dad was in a coma for weeks. Mom broke both her legs and hip. I couldn't have left them. I haven't. Until now."

"Family is the most important thing in our lives. Without them, we are lost."

Lauren reached her hand up and gently touched his cheek. She stroked his unshaven jawline and memorized every subtle change from what she'd remembered.

"Our hearts would have been broken, no matter what. We both would have chosen our families over our love."

Marc nodded while he stepped towards her. He took the shoes from her hand and threw them back on the beach, and then pulled her close.

"But what we have...it's more than just a memory of a love."

She loved being in his arms. It was everything she'd remembered it to be. But...even though this is what she'd wanted, what she'd hoped would happen, why did it feel wrong? Like it wasn't meant to be?

There was a sadness in her heart that surprised her.

"I'm not sure if it is." She hated the words as she spoke them, but she knew, in her heart, it was the truth.

"If there is one thing that I've learned about myself, it is that my heart is never wrong. Ever. I loved you. I loved everything about you, or what I thought I knew about you. And I held that close. It's what got me through these past six years. The memory of what we had. The memory of our love. And it was enough. More than enough. But, that's all it was—"

"Don't say it." Marc shook his head but wouldn't look her in the eyes.

She ran her fingers over his jawline and then touched his lips.

"It was just a memory." She stood on her tiptoes and kissed him. A gentle touch of her lips against his.

A goodbye.

"It wasn't just a memory. What we had was real," Marc argued.

She stepped out of his arms. "It was real. Then. But for the past six years...it's just been a memory. We're not the same people we were then. We've grown up, changed...but we're still very much apart."

"We don't have to be though." Marc stuck his hands in his pockets. "You've given up on us, on the idea of us. I can hear it in your voice."

Lauren didn't say anything. What could she say?

"This weekend wasn't meant for us to say goodbye. It was to give us a second chance. Sure, there are obstacles...but I knew the moment Lexi showed me your picture that we'd been given a second chance."

"Don't you think that's a sign, though? That we share best friends and yet, in all those years, we've never crossed each other's path? Marc, I deal with your company on a regular basis and we never put two and two together. Doesn't that say something?"

For two heartbeats, there was silence. Lauren could have sworn that time stopped between them as she waited for him to answer.

"It means we weren't ready."

She heard the hope in his voice, the belief, and tears pricked her eyes. She turned from him and stared out over the water. She tilted her head back and stared up into the cloudless sky before she closed her eyes.

"Every year, on the weekend of when I last saw you, I hide myself away so that I can remember you. Every other day of the year, I've forced myself to move on, to forget you, but once a year, I remember what we had. I remember what it was like to feel loved, to be in your arms, to believe in a future together despite all the odds. I try to recreate our meals. I write you letters...I fall in love with you all over again."

His arms encircled around her and she leaned back

into his chest. She rested her head on his shoulder and breathed in deep, letting this moment envelope her.

"Don't forget about me, please," Marc whispered in her ear.

"I had planned on letting you go, this weekend." Her voice broke against her own whispered words and Marc's arms tightened around her.

"I'm not letting you," he said. "Ever again."

"But what if I want you to?" It was hard to say the words, to admit them. Her heart broke a little and the tears flowed down her cheeks. But she couldn't take them back.

Marc laid a kiss on the top of her head and then rested his cheek there.

They stood there, for what seemed like hours, but was probably only minutes. Lauren revealed in each second and knew she would always remember this moment. She would hold it close to her heart and think of how it felt to have his arms around her once more, when she laid in bed at night, alone.

"You are my soul mate, Lauren Summer," Marc whispered. "That will never change. There will never be another in my heart. But if you want to walk away, if you need to say goodbye to me, to us..." his voice faltered, "then I will not stop you."

She turned in his arms then, not believing what he'd just said. She'd thought...she thought he would have fought harder for her. For them. But he wasn't.

And she wanted him to. Needed him to...except, wasn't that what she'd said earlier?

"I will always be here. Always. But I will not force you to do anything you are not ready to do. Yet. I've lost six years without you in my life, but I will gladly lose another six if it means you will keep thinking of me, knowing that I haven't walked away." He leaned down and placed a kiss on her forehead, then on her closed eyes, and then on her lips, where he stayed, his lips moving over hers in a silent plea.

"Just promise me you will never forget about me." He breathed the words into her mouth as he laid one final kiss on her lips and then stepped away.

She was so confused. What just happened?

She wiped at the tears that lingered on her cheeks and shook her head, not sure what to say or what to do. So she did the only thing she knew...she ran.

Marc watched Lauren run from him. As difficult as it was for him to stand still, he did it.

He knew this is what she needed to do.

They'd have to work on this habit, though; it wasn't going to go well if she continually ran from him when she was confused.

He moved upwards, away from the water, and sat down in the sand. He wasn't sure how long he would have to wait for her to come back, so he might as well do what he wanted for a bit.

And right now, sitting on the beach, soaking in the sun, was exactly what he wanted.

"Is Eden still the paradise you pictured it to be?" Someone stepped over him and blocked out the sun.

Marc turned. His hand shielded his eyes and he glared up at Sean.

"Mind if I join you?" Sean asked as he sat down beside him. "Saw Lauren running. All okay?"

Marc shrugged. "She's got to work things out, but she'll be back. Hopefully."

"I don't know, man. That's twice she's run from you in a matter of days. Hours, actually. I'd be a bit worried, if I were in your shoes."

Marc leaned back on his elbows and smiled. "She'll come back." He knew she would. He wasn't too worried. He didn't know why...but there was a sense of...peace about all of this.

"My brothers and I are going to get a game of beach volleyball going. You want in?" Sean pushed himself up to his feet.

There was nothing Marc liked better than a good game of volleyball on the beach, but not today.

"I told her I'd be here, waiting. Don't want to break my promise."

Sean reached his hand down and Marc grabbed hold of it and shook it. "You're a good man. We're all rooting for you," Sean said.

"Even Tyler?"

"Well," Sean grinned, "Tyler's rooting for Lauren. Can't blame the guy either."

Marc laughed as Sean left. No, he couldn't blame the guy at all.

🍿🍿🍿

Lauren could barely see where she was going from the steady stream of tears in her eyes. She was a fool. Again.

Why was the first thing she thought to do was to run? Why? She wasn't a runner—in life or in character—so why did she take off from Marc instead of facing things like a grown woman would do?

Soul mates. The word bloomed in her heart while at the same time planted a seed of fear.

Up ahead she could see some activity. There were tables, chairs, umbrellas, hammocks, a game of volleyball and little cabanas all over the place.

She slowed and wiped her face. She hoped she didn't look like the ugly crying fool she was.

She couldn't believe she ran. Again. He was bound to think her emotionally unstable and he'd be right.

She needed to get a hold of herself and stop reacting when what she should do is live. Live in the moment. Trust her heart, herself. This wasn't like her and if Melanie were here, she'd probably get a stern talking-to and the chocolate back in her room would be hijacked.

She made her way past all the groups that stood there and tried to hide her smile as she saw the obvious triplets in the crowds. For the umpteenth time, she wished her sisters were here with her. She needed to remember to get the info for this triplet group from Tyler before she left.

Ahead of her was a small cabana-like building where there were. Back at home, she'd never have a drink until at least mid-afternoon, but here, she honestly couldn't care less. Maybe it would help her calm down, soothe her soul.

Maybe.

She couldn't stop her smile as she read over the list on the chalkboard. Jamaican Me Crazy? She needed to get that for Marc. Then she spotted it—Eden's Miracle Cure. That's exactly what she needed—a miracle. And it came with chocolate!

Lauren stood next to a woman who looked at the list as well.

"A chocolate drink?" Lauren said beneath her breath.

"I know." The woman laughed. "I just ordered it. I mean, how can it be bad?"

Lauren liked how this woman thought. "I know, right?"

She watched as the woman beside her raised her hand to the bartender and asked him to make a second before she turned to Lauren.

"I'm Carissa."

"Lauren."

The two women shook hands, and then grinned gleefully when the bartender set their drinks down in front of them. Tapping glasses in unspoken cheers, they each took a sip.

Lauren sighed. The tension left her body as the smooth, sweet chocolate slid down her throat with a trail of delicious heat in its wake.

"Oh my..." she managed to say while at the same time Carissa muttered, "Thank God."

"That bad?" Lauren set her drink down on the counter.

Carissa shrugged. "I'm here on a platonic vacation with my best friend. Problem is he wants to delete the platonic part and turn this week into forever."

"Wow." At least she wasn't the only one here not finding Eden to be the promised land of paradise right now.

"Yeah."

"And I gather you're not interested in him romantically?"

Carissa took another sip of her drink. "Truthfully, I...well...I mean..."

"Ah. So you are." She took back her earlier

thought.

Carissa nodded. "I think I am. But he's never glanced my way once back home in the six years we've been friends. I'm afraid it's the romantic atmosphere of this island that's got him all hot and bothered. What if I give in, then we go home and he realizes I'm not the woman of his dreams after all?"

"Do you really think that's what will happen?"

"No," Carissa admitted, "I don't."

The thought of love, romance, and going home forced Lauren to reach for her glass and take a gulp of her drink.

"Looks like I'm not the only one freaking out," Carissa said softly.

Lauren gave her a rueful grin. "You're not. Do you believe in soul mates?"

Without giving Carissa a chance to respond, Lauren took another gulp of her drink, and then set it down.

"I do. Or did. Or do."

"Which is it?" Carissa asked.

"I do." Lauren shrugged. She could be honest here. What did it matter? "I'm here because the guy who I believe is my soul mate wants to reconnect."

"And that's a bad thing?"

"No, well...maybe?" Lauren shook her head. "I don't know. Honestly, I'm so confused at this point. I mean, I've been in love with this guy for six years, but what if I've only been pining after a memory? Is that even possible? He seems to be too good to be real."

"Is it possible that it is real?"

Lauren quirked her lips and glanced behind her.

"That's what scares me," she admitted. "I came here to say goodbye but I find myself falling head over heels again, just like before." She finished the last of her drink and pushed the glass forward.

"If my sisters were here, you know what they'd tell me?"

Carissa shook her head but Lauren could tell she was interested.

"They'd tell me to take a chance. To trust in love."

"Sounds like good advice."

Lauren turned around and rested her elbows on the back of the bar while she looked up into the clear blue sky. She wished they were here, to help her, to give her confidence.

"Tell you what. Pretend I'm one of your sisters. But instead of telling you to trust in love, I'm going to tell you to trust your heart."

Lauren turned her head and smiled at Carissa. She liked her.

"Then I'm going to do the same. Trust your own heart and see what happens." Lauren pushed herself away from the bar. "Hopefully we'll run into each other again," she said before she walked back to where she'd left Marc.

Trust her heart. Nothing scared her more while excited her at the same time.

What was her heart telling her?

She thought back to how comfortable she felt in his presence, how all she could think about was Marc's arms around her, how light her heart felt when she'd made the decision late last night to give their love a second chance.

There were so many obstacles, so many reasons this couldn't work, why it wouldn't...but was she willing to go through another year, two, or even another six, wondering what if? What if she'd given it a try? What if it had worked?

She made her way back down the beach and couldn't believe that Marc was still there, where she'd left him.

He must have noticed her approach because by the time she was even remotely close to him, he was waiting for her.

"Are you done running, love?"

"How long would you have waited for me?" Her heart pounded in her chest and she wasn't sure whether she could wait for his answer.

"However long you needed." He reached for her hands and pulled her close until there was barely any space left between them.

"I shouldn't have run, again."

He only smiled at her, but his eyes were a brilliant

green and the message in them told her everything she needed to know.

"You live on the other side of the ocean." There were so many obstacles between them.

"I do." He nodded.

"And I don't travel much with my job, so it's not like I could just take off to come and see you."

"I understand. Paul also likes to keep me chained to my desk, running his company for him."

"Long-distance relationships don't always work..." Her voice drifted off as she realized how futile her arguments really were.

"Did you say that to Lexi when she gave you the same arguments between her and Paul?" Marc had a teasing glint in his gaze.

She shook her head. "You know I didn't."

"Then give us a chance. That's all I ask. Just a chance." His grip tightened against hers.

"And if it doesn't work?" That was her biggest fear.

He pulled her close. "It will. I haven't waited six years for it not to work."

She gazed into his eyes and knew, in that moment, that she could not only trust her heart, but she could trust him with it.

"Okay," she said.

"Okay?" He sounded surprised.

"I'm willing if you are."

A huge grin spread across his face at her words and he pulled her in tight and held her close.

"I have a surprise for you," he whispered into her ear.

"I like surprises," she said.

"I know." He let go of her and started to walk, pulling her along with him.

"Where are we going?" She almost had to run, which was difficult to do in the sand.

"If I told you, then it wouldn't be a surprise, would it?"

"Can you give me a hint at least?"

Marc stopped suddenly and she ran into him. "Do you trust me?"

She nodded.

He turned and waved his arm at one of the brothers who sat in a golf cart up on the path. The brother waved back and Marc turned to her.

"Let's go." He had a huge smile on his face.

She followed along, unsure of what the plan was, but once they reached the cart, Trevor hopped out so there was room for both her and Marc in the front.

"Everything is set up," Trevor said.

"Thanks. Any special requests?"

Trevor shook his head. "Any will do."

Lauren sat there, confused but before she could ask any questions, Marc started the golf cart and drove.

He reached across and held her hand and that's

how they sat, for the next ten minutes, until they drove up to the main door of the castle. The whole trip, as the building loomed ahead, Lauren's mouth dropped and she couldn't believe what she saw.

"It's amazing, isn't it?" Marc helped her out of the cart and they walked up the stone steps that led to the main door.

"Breathtaking," she replied. She couldn't get over the expansive size of the building.

The massive wood door to the castle opened up as they climbed to the top of the stairs and Marc led her inside. She smiled at a staff member who stood there as they passed by.

"Where are we going?"

"Just wait and see."

Lauren barely had time to see all the wondrous sights around her, from the marbled floor to the vases that overflowed with fresh flowers. They stopped in front of a set of elevator doors and Marc pushed the button.

"I need you to close your eyes."

"I'm sorry?"

The boyish grin on Marc's face grew. "Will you close your eyes, please?"

Lauren slowly closed her eyes and heard the ding of doors as they opened. He led her inside and put his arms around her so that she could lean back against him.

"I hope you like my surprise," he whispered in her ear.

"Can I open my eyes now?"

"No." He chuckled.

They stood there and listened to the soft elevator music. Lauren couldn't help but wonder where they were going.

At last the elevator doors opened and Marc led her out and then they walked, and walked. Marc was gentle as he instructed her to climb a few stairs, to watch out for a table or two but the whole time he wouldn't let her open her eyes.

Finally they stopped. A soft breeze billowed around her and caressed her skin.

"Okay, you can open them now."

When she did, she was breathless. They stood high up on a balcony and overlooked the island below. Soft white clouds floated in the distance over the ocean and the trees swayed in the wind.

And Marc stood at her side, taking it all in.

"The heights—are you okay?" She knew he was afraid of heights and couldn't believe he stood there, at the edge of the balcony, with her.

He squeezed her hand and leaned forward, until his elbows rested on the railing. "It's beautiful, isn't it?"

"It's amazing. But..."

He turned and looked at her. "You had wanted to climb to the top of the Eiffel Tower so badly but didn't because I was too afraid to. After you left, I made myself a promise to never to do that to you again...so I faced my fear. It took me awhile, but the next time you come to Paris, I'll climb those stairs with you."

Lauren blinked away tears she hadn't realized gathered in her eyes.

"I...I..." She sighed, unable to form words to describe what she felt. Overwhelmed at the beauty before them, amazed at the strength of the man in front of her, honored that he would do something like that for her...and thrilled that he'd done all this for her.

"I wanted this weekend to be about you. A time where you felt spoiled and loved. A time when you could relax and let others take care of you rather than you taking care of others. I wanted..." Marc paused and looked out over the view. "I wanted to show you that you deserve all this and so much more."

He wiped the tears that fell along her skin and then bent down to kiss her. It was soft, full of promise and love, and it was enough. Enough for her, for her heart.

"I have one more surprise, when you are ready to leave this gorgeous view."

Lauren laughed. "I'm not sure I'll ever want to leave this. It's breathtaking."

Marc rolled his eyes. "What if I said we could come back and have dinner here, on the balcony, and watch the sun set?"

"That would be perfect." It sounded amazing and very romantic.

"Good." He bent down and kissed her again. "We need to go back to our rooms. That box you were given last night—you're going to need it for my next surprise."

CHAPTER NINE

Forget the hammocks and the massages and all the amazing clothes in her closet.

Forget even the fact that this whole weekend was all because of Marc.

This moment was something she would never forget.

Her. Marc. Hands covered in chocolate.

Thank goodness she'd changed before coming. Marc wouldn't let her open the box from last night until almost the last second.

Inside the box was a brown apron with an adorable chocolate saying embroidered on it.

All you need is love, but a little chocolate now and then doesn't hurt.

She loved it.

He'd arranged a private chocolate making

afternoon with the island's own private chocolatier.

"I still can't believe Paul gave his best-selling chocolates to this Master dude as exclusives when he's got his own chocolatier on the island," Marc grumbled as he poured his chocolate into small molds.

"I can't believe I've got two of those boxes now in my room."

Marc's head lifted. "Pardon?"

"I've got two boxes of those chocolates in my room," she repeated.

"Well, that little..." Marc's lips thinned and he shook his head.

"Let me guess." Lauren tapped her mold tray to get rid of any little bubbles. "You didn't get any."

She smiled and knew she'd need to thank Paul when she got back home.

"Will you share?" There was a hopeful note in Marc's voice.

"Um, hello? You work for the guy. Can't you get your own?"

"Trust me, I've tried. Paul hand makes each box himself before he seals them and gets me to print a shipping label. I don't even get the throwaways."

"Paul Ormand is a master all on his own," their chocolatier said as he cleaned up the workspace. "I had the opportunity to watch him once...it's why I am in this profession today."

Marc took both his and her trays to the fridge

section and set them inside. "Any way you can get your hands on one of his gold boxes?"

"Oh, leave him alone, Marc. I happen to have a box that's meant for the both of us anyways." She gave him a wink before she headed to the sink to wash her hands. As she watched the chocolate melt away under the hot water, she thought about the box she'd found on her bedside table earlier.

It was the message written on it, specifically, that made her smile.

Share.

After an afternoon of surprises and laughter while they created their own chocolates, Lauren had no problem sharing that box of chocolates with Marc.

Lauren wasn't sure how much time she had left on the island, but she wasn't sure she even wanted to leave. This was the perfect place for her and Marc to reconnect, to get to know each other all over again and to build something that could last.

Last a lifetime.

Wouldn't that be nice? She knew it would take some work—okay, it would take a lot of work—but it would be worth it. She'd rather try to build something with him over spending another month, week, or even day without him in her life.

It was amazing really. They'd met six years ago and over a week, they knew they had something special. Something so special that it was like a seed, fermented in their heart, and waited for the right moment to sprout and bloom.

Arms wrapped around her waist and she smiled.

"So you'll share, huh?" Marc placed a small kiss on her cheek.

"I might," she gave a little shrug, "if you're nice."

"We made chocolate together, we're about to have dinner watching the sunset, and we can sit in front of the fire tonight making s'mores with the chocolate bars we made today. Isn't that nice enough?" Marc nuzzled the side of her neck and tickled her.

"And to think I almost didn't come."

"What?"

"When the invitation arrived, I thought it was meant for Jessica. I told Joely that the invitation needed to be returned."

"Your sister knew, though."

"I still can't believe you set this all up."

"I had some help. We have some great friends who believe in the power of love."

Lauren smiled. "I'm so happy they're back together. Their's is a love meant to last a lifetime."

"They're not the only one." Marc turned her around and kissed her with a passion she knew she'd never forget.

114

Dear Reader,

Thank you for taking the time to read Return to Sender? I hope you enjoyed my sweet romance, and that you recognized characters from my Decadent Event series set in Banff, Alberta.

Over the past few years, I've received emails have meant the world to me in more ways than you can imagine. Thank you for sharing your stories with me on loved ones you have lost, I am honored and blessed with your trust. If you have left a review for one of my books - thank you.

If you haven't signed up yet, I have a newsletter where I share my favorite recipes, news on my books, special gifts and more! If you haven't, sign up today – you can find out more about my newsletter, secret society and more on my website.

To find out more about my books, available titles, new releases and upcoming stories, visit my website - www.SteenaHolmes.com.

I look forward to getting to know you!

Steena

OTHER BOOKS BY STEENA HOLMES

~

The Memory Child

Stillwater Bay Series:
Before the Storm
Stillwater Rising
Finding Emma Series:
Finding Emma
Dear Jack
Emma's Secret
Dottie's Memories
Decadent Events Series:
Sweet Memories
Sweet Dreams

ABOUT THE AUTHOR

Steena Holmes is a self-proclaimed chocoholic, an avid reader and now a NY Times & *USA Today* bestselling author with over 1 million copies of her books sold.

She grew up in a small town in Canada and holds a bachelor's degree in theology. She is the author of eleven novels and novellas, including *Finding Emma*, for which she was awarded a National Indie Excellence Book Award in 2012.

If you would like to stay informed on Steena's new released, please visit her website and sign up for her newsletter. www.SteenaHolmes.com

SWEET MEMORIES
Book One

Happily-ever-after only happens once in a lifetime, right? But what if Prince Charming runs for the hills at the first sign of trouble and leaves you to pick up the pieces.

Thinking her marriage was over, Tessa was more than a little shocked to fall into the arms of her husband (literally) at a party she'd planned through her new company, Decadent Events. When he asks her out for coffee, she assumes it's to sign the divorce papers he'd seen.

What's a girl to do when her heart still goes pitter-patter for a man who ran out on her six months after they made their forever vows but comes back asking for another chance?

DECADENT EVENT, BOOK TWO

SWEET DREAMS
Book Two

Since chocolate couldn't cure her broken heart, creating the finest croissants this side of Paris would have to do. Who needed love anyways?

Opening up Sweet Treats could have been the answer to all her problems - except all the problems she'd ran away from in Paris followed after her, via a first class ticket and wore rugged jeans. It didn't help he made the best chocolates she'd ever tasted, either.

What's a girl to do when the only man she'd ever loved was willing to give their love another try - even when she'd been the one to betray any hope they'd had at a happily-ever-after. She knew she'd made a horrible mistake keeping her past a secret, but now that it was out in the open, could they move past it?

From NYT Bestselling author comes her latest novella in the Decadent Events Series that you won't want to miss. If you love the fine things in life - specifically a buttery croissant, melt-in-your-mouth chocolate and a sweet love that endures, you'll enjoy Sweet Dreams.